I0591955

Lawrence Anderson

Safehaven
Reunion

C. I. Anderson

VILLAGE BOOKS INDEPENDENT PUBLISHING PROGRAM

BELLINGHAM, WASHINGTON

Second Edition
Copyright ©2019 Ilene Anderson

All Rights Reserved.
No part of this book may be reproduced, scanned, or
distributed in any printed or electronic form without
permission from the author. The author shall neither have
liability nor responsibility to anyone with respect to any loss
or damage caused by the information contained in this
book either directly or indirectly.

All characters are fictional.

Sculptures used in the story are true sculptures that are located on
the campus of Western Washington University. Please visit: https://
bellinghamwalks.com/2017/07/21/the-western-washington-university-
outdoor-sculpture-collection-walk/

Art and Illustrations by Lawrence Anderson and Hans C. Anderson

Printed and bound in the United States of America
First edition printed ©July 2019

Published by Village Books Independent Publishing Program
1200 11th Street
Bellingham, WA 98225
Tel: 360-671-2626

Acknowledgments

To Fairhaven College and all the dedicated and enlightened professors and staff who helped me become who I am. I will never forget you.

To all my teachers and mentors who supported my educational and personal development. I can never repay your service.

To my parents, Larry and Sharon. To my sisters, Joan, Cheryl Karen. To my nieces, Shannon and Caitlin.

To Alan, Arlynn, Kathy, Dean, Corbin, Verna, Curt, and all of my predecessors, whose influence was immeasurable. You have made the world a better place.

To my cousins in the Chicago area who were willing to read my rough draft.

To all of my animal helpers, who taught me the most basic and important principles of life. Knowing them made me a better person. Special thanks to Sam, Langston, Sebastian, Harlie, Dora and Hugo.

To all my friends who supported me, especially Eric and Yvette

In celebration of Fairhaven College 50th Anniversary.

Ilene lives and works in the Pacific Northwest. She earned her Bachelor's Degree from Fairhaven College, Bellingham and her Master's Degree in Psychology from Antioch University, Seattle. She is working on her second book of the Safehaven series.

Other special thanks to Lee, Donna and Cat

CHAPTERS

Chapter 1

Friday Evening

Lawrence Anderson

I put down my pen, close my notebook and carefully put away my laptop. I look at the clock and realize I have been writing for two hours. I'm not a writer but feel the need to write this story that is unraveling out of me. Every night I am in the same place, this special place that is unknown, yet familiar. It is my nighttime home, the one I always return to in my dreams.

I look into the mirror that is hanging near the front door of my Cedar Crest home. I stop to plump my dishwater blonde curls and outline my eyeliner with my index finger. The eyeliner brings out my blue-green eyes. I look good enough. I turn to yell a last goodbye to my children, my sister and our cats. I rush to my SUV that is parked in the long driveway, throw my suitcase in and hurriedly drive off. I don't want to be late.

I arrive in the city of Baypoint a little after 5 pm on a Friday night. It's a warm and sunny evening and I can smell the marine air coming off of the bay. I am happy to be back at Safehaven College. Safehaven is a small college and one of the many colleges that make up Wasgard University. I am attending my thirty-year reunion. Both Safehaven and Wasgard have yearly reunions which I religiously attend, however, this year is special as it is Safehaven's 50th year anniversary.

I originally chose to attend Safehaven College because of its' unique style of learning and social values. The college prides itself on its philosophy of learning. Per Safehaven, learning should be for the pleasure of learning, not forced memorization and regurgitation of useless information that cannot be applied. The college encourages its' students to step out of prescribed roles and expectations. Experimentation is supported and failure is considered a learning opportunity. Therefore, I was not bound to traditional fields of study, social norms or methods of learning. This was such a relief. Safehaven College was established in the 1960's and was greatly influenced by the 60's culture. So, it's not a surprise that many of Safehaven's students are politically active because "personal is political."

I take pleasure remembering my college years. These were the years when I came alive. After moving out of my parent's home, emancipating myself, I opened up to the possibility of who I may become. The options where endless. This was my opportunity to explore and find myself.

As I walk onto campus, I gaze at the green trees and smell the clean air. This causes more waves of memories to crash over me. I am taken by old feelings of optimism. College is the place where one can claim their destiny. I visualize the students thirty years ago, sitting on the grass, meeting by the campus sculptures before and after class, laughing and conversing, overwhelmed with the optimism of youth.

Those days are gone now, leaving only memories. Memories of my first love, the pain of the break-up and the many break-ups that followed. The memories of my first time being intoxicated, exploring the beaches and parks in the area that are within walking distance from the campus. I remember the feeling of exhilaration as I learned something new in class that finally supplied the missing piece of knowledge that made sense of the world.

Later, I would realize the disappointment of discovering the world is not always a fair or equitable place. Now, I no longer believe that I can be anyone or anything I want to be. Though, I still believe "knowledge is power." Safehaven taught me to be aware and I have become painfully aware of the difference between theory and application. How does one take the coveted philosophy that is learned in higher education and apply it to everyday life? I'm still working on this and struggling with how to integrate ideal values into the world and our culture.

Throughout my life, I have heard of and learned about extraordinary people but I know they are just that, extra- ordinary. I had some extraordinary professors at Safehaven, whom I love and admire but the question still remains. How can I apply this to my everyday life?

Wasgard University's campus is very spread out and Safehaven is at the far end of the campus. I reach a small familiar hill that leads to the college and the dormitory where I will be spending my weekend. I'm grateful the college offers returning students an affordable, yet comfortable place to stay. It is much better than staying at a motel.

I will stay in the same dorm room I lived in as a student. I walk up to and slowly read the sign above the dorm entrance "Sojourner Truth Hall" and reminisce. I check in with the Residential Assistant and I am given a key for room #9. The room has a good view of the little pond that sits between the brick walkways that lead to the dorm. The dorm faces inward toward campus. As a student, the positioning of the dorms made me feel safe and protected from the real world outside of academia.

I arrive earlier than the other returning students. My roommate has not yet arrived. I wonder who it will be this year. I feel a tinge of excitement thinking about seeing my fellow classmates again. I think of who I was during my college years and who I have since become. I am different from who I expected to be. The unfolding of my self has been both pleasant and surprising. At my age, I am more comfortable with this unfolding and experience it with an open mind rather than something to be horrified and embarrassed by, like when I was younger.

After using my key to open my dorm room, I guess Safehaven hasn't digitalized yet, I throw my suitcase onto the twin bed which is standard furnish in the dorms. The small room is chilly. The current students are out for summer break, so the rooms are not yet up to temperature.

Although amenities are slight in the dorms, it always catches me off guard just how small the rooms really are. There is no place to cook and only a small refrigerator in the corner of the room. I smile to myself as I plug it in and it starts to hum. The dorm fridge saved me from the cafeteria meals and the associated gastrointestinal distress. The entrees in the cafeteria that I could eat without digestive disturbance seemed to put on the pounds, almost magically. I remember how I gained 10 pounds in the first month on the cafeteria food.

Thankfully I have been a devote athlete all my life. I played on the first female soccer team in my city and before that played American football with the boys in the backyards of our neighborhood. Back then girls could not play football or most of the other sports. Thank God for Title IX (and Billy Jean King's Women's Sports Foundation to monitor its compliance). Anyway, sports helped me control the weight gain typical of first year students.

As I look out the window, I can see the cafeteria located one story below Safehaven College. It's reeving up for the alumni that will soon be convening on the campus. Below the cafeteria is one of my favorite spots as a student. The lower level has a lounge with couches, a sound system and good views of the pond and patio outside. I used to gather with my classmates here, drink coffee, talk and express new ideas and philosophies. On weekends, we had special gatherings, sometimes there was music, other times literary readings or speeches but my favorite were the dances.

The cold winter nights in Baypoint generally prohibit going outside. However, on the late spring nights, temperatures allowed the students to make their way from the lounge to the outside patio area. These nights were such a relief after the long winter weather that kept us hostage indoors. Once spring broke it was hard to go back indoors.

Safehaven believes in preserving our natural settings, "Live within nature, not against it." I used to love walking under the old trees on campus and the adjoining nature reserve called Conundrum Hill. As a student, I regularly ran under these trees, filling my lungs with the sweet, fresh air. As I look toward the hill, I realize the trees were old then but they haven't changed much. I breathe in the same sweet smells from the trees.

I close the slightly opened window in the dorm. I want to give the room a chance to warm up before bedtime. I unpack the snacks I brought with me. I pull out some garlic hummus and vegetables and place them in the fridge. I always pack health food when I'm on the road. I subconsciously look around in a self-conscious way, as I pull out a bottle of organic Zinfandel wine. The university's campus is a "dry" campus. Not everyone paid attention to this rule. Most of the students in the dorms are under twenty-one years of age which is the legal drinking age. Certainly, there are many colleges and universities that have a reputation for partying and Wasgard was no exception. Although, Safehaven typically were more marijuana smokers than drinkers. I will keep my organic Zinfandel a secret, just in case I am breaking any rules.

I hear the jostling of a key in the door. The noise automatically makes me look up toward the door. Whoever is trying to open the door is having a very difficult time getting their key to work. I jump up to investigate. As I open the door, I am face to face with a woman who looks vaguely familiar. The facial features and the dark curly hair remind me of someone I used to know but not a regular to the yearly reunions. "Lawren is that you?" "Andi is that you?" We both exclaim at the same time. Lawren timidly announces, "I don't think my key works." I look closely at her key jacket and notice it is for room #10 "I think you have the wrong room." "Oh, I guess I wasn't paying attention. I must be exhausted from traveling." We both laugh." "It looks like you are in the adjacent room."

The dorms are set up so that each room has two residents who share a bathroom with the next double room. "It looks like we'll be sharing the bathroom at least." I become surprisingly aware of how strikingly beautiful Lawren is. She appears to have improved with age. Her green eyes draw me in. I say "Here, let me help you with your luggage. Where are you traveling from?" "California" she says.

"I recently moved there to take an Assistant Professor position at UC Santa Cruz. I am teaching Law and Society to first-year law students." Lawren asks, "Where are you living?" "Oh, I am living in a small town called Cedar Crest. It is a suburb and I'm a Private Investigator." I continue, "I was thinking about attending Santa Cruz in my twenties but didn't want to go straight through for a Ph. D. Instead, I earned my Master's Degree in Psychology at a private university in Seattle." I carry Lawren's luggage to dorm #10 by going through the shared bathroom. I set it down in the cold dorm room. "Your room is cold also. Are you going to dinner tonight? I hear it is spaghetti with tofu or turkey meatballs, peasant bread, a garden salad and wine. It will be nice to eat in the cafeteria again, even though the food always made me sick." "Yeah", says Lawren. "A lot of good memories. It is really nice seeing you again. See you at dinner." I catch myself feeling excited as I close the shared bathroom door to room #10.

Dinner is at 5:00 pm. The same time it was 30 years ago. Many of times I have made the journey from my dorm up the long set of stairs to the cafeteria, in order to partake in the "barfing breakfast", "lingering lunch" and the "diarrhea dinners" that were offered to the students. I wonder if the university food has taken any years off my life. I think the university put so many stairs up to the cafeteria to offset the effects of their high fat, low quality food.

I finally reach the top of the stairs, being a bit out of breath. I hear the familiar clanking of silverware, plates and glasses that is characteristic of institutional kitchens. In the background, I hear the faint sound of drums and the strumming of guitars. In the spirit of Safehaven there is usually a musical improvisation circle. Today is no exception. To the side of the cafeteria is a large circle of chairs, many of which are unclaimed. The open chairs have some sort of instrument sitting on them, welcoming and encouraging former students to join in. I usually play the drums, as I have very little musical talent and can fake it with drums. There is also an upright piano sitting next to the circle.

One of our former students, who is also my friend, was well known at Safehaven for her piano playing skills. I hoped Juni would show up tonight to play in the improv circle. Juni is a beautiful African American woman with dark, coffee colored skin and deep-set brown eyes. Her smile is inviting. She came from a long line of musicians in her family. Her father moved the family to Washington from the South, hoping Juni would have better opportunity and less adversity in the Northwest.

Our college is known for encouraging the arts. In the past, Juni has performed at numerous "Art Fairs" that are a regular occurrence at Safehaven. Juni earned her Bachelor's Degree in Business and Economics then went on to earn her Master's Degree in Business at an Ivy League university. She now works for the State of Washington in Seattle.

Safehaven wanted to recreate our younger days, so all reunion guests are issued a meal card for their meals. As a student, I always lost my meal card and had to go all the way to Main Campus to get it re-issued. Sometimes I didn't want to make the effort, so I just ate off other dorm residents' meal trays. This would make me feel like a vagabond so, eventually I would make the trip across campus. The staff at Student Services knew me by name.

Tonight, I feel hungry. Therefore, the improv circle will have to wait until after dinner...and wine. The food smells almost appetizing but how can you ruin spaghetti? I walk toward the same table my friends and I always sit at, as students and alumni. The table is close to the windows overlooking the patio. Here we have a good view of the trees outside while having a good view of everyone in the dining hall. It looks like I am the first at our table to arrive for dinner.

On the other side of the dining hall is a wine bar. I start off with a red blend. Thankfully the university got a good deal on some local wine. I whirl the wine in its clear plastic cup, I breathe in, allowing the aroma to excite my sense of smell then deliberately take a sip, fancying the excitation of my taste buds. Using this method, I finish two glasses on an empty stomach. I notice I feel a little lightheaded as I get up to walk toward the bathroom. I can always tell I am drunk once I stand up. Unfortunately, by this time, it's too late. I carefully maneuver my way, trying to be careful not to lose my balance in front of others in the dining hall. I've always been a lightweight drinker. This came in handy as a student because I could not afford to drink much anyway.

The bathrooms are down the hall and to the right. As I walk, I feel like those mice in the research experiment where the malevolent doctor cuts out part of their brain then has them run a maze. The point of the experiment was to find out what area of their brain held memory. In the end, the mad doctor cuts out most of their brain but the mice were still able to find their way through the maze without exception. Same for me, I knew this campus drunk or sober.

The bathroom is the same color it has always been, peach and light tan. Inside the women's bathroom are the same old writings on the walls, though the content is slightly different. Comments are written in different styles, some angry, some in soft optimistic tones, but all have socio-political themes. The quote written on the stall door in front of me, as I sit down on the toilet, reads, "A woman is like a tea bag. You never know how strong she is until she gets in hot water. -- Eleanor Roosevelt." As I reach for the toilet paper, I see another quote, "Women have always been an equal part of the past. We just haven't been part of history. -- Gloria Steinem." In red ink and on the left side of the stall is "Each person must live their life as a model for others. -- Rosa Parks." Then, on the right side of the stall, another quote "You are sitting on a gold mine. -- My Grandmother." I chuckle to myself.

As I return to my table, more sober then when I left, I can see that Harley and Lexa have arrived. They are sitting at the improv circle. Harley is laughing at Lexa. Lexa is beating on a hand drum in an uncoordinated fashion. Her straight blondish-red hair is thrashing about as she comes down on the drums. Her contribution to the circle is in a rhythm and tempo that does not match the others playing in the circle. I think back and remember the lip-sync nights at a local bar during our college years. Lexa's singing is even worse than her drumming abilities. She sings off key and has no idea of beat. This trait is enduring and entertaining. Thankfully she is not sensitive to laughter at her expense. Nothing a drink, or two, can't remedy. I stop by the bar and pick up a couple glasses of wine and a bottle of beer. I sit down by the two and hand each a drink, saving the last one for myself.

Lexa accepts her beer, winks at me with her bright blue eyes and drinks straight out of the bottle. She has always said beer tastes better out of the bottle rather than a glass. Lexa smiles then gives me a big hug. I realize how much I enjoy her company. Lexa played for the university's basketball team and was largely responsible for leading them to the championships. She is naturally good at all sports but especially good at basketball. After she graduated from college, she played for the local women's semiprofessional basketball team. Her career ended after about five years of play. She was tired of the stress of traveling and competing. After she retired, she was offered a coaching position on her former team which eventually became one of the first women's professional teams. She still travels a lot during the season but this lacks the additional stress of competition.

I look over at Harley. She has grown her hair out. Her dark brown waves of hair coil as they sit on her shoulders. Her light brown eyes stand out. She takes a sip of her wine and nods a thank you. Her mood is relaxed. Harley is from an affluent family. Both of her parents were medical doctors. She fortunately inherited her parent's brains but not their perfectionism and work ethic. She renounced her parent's values in part by attending Safehaven College. Safehaven is the opposite of the Ivy League school her parents attended. They experienced the 1960's but did not participate in the 60's culture. Harley is their only child and is the hippie they never were. Harley participates in the counter culture by being an activist and holds liberal values her parents feel uneasy about. They are much too concerned about what others may think or how their position in society may suffer. Harley's parents aren't embarrassed by her but just can't understand her.

It was as if we were young again, laughing without a care in the world. Time standing still. It didn't matter that we had to wait in a long line for dinner. We talk and catch up with each other. We are together again and this is all that matters. We sit down at our table after getting another round of drinks. The spaghetti is bland. I add salt and garlic powder. I pass these condiments around the table without asking, knowing others will like to improve the taste of their meal. We toast to our reunion, then toast to our health, our future, prosperity and anything else we can think of. We are being optimistic and forgetting for the moment that we are older and our lives have become much more complicated since college.

We have all been in and out of relationships. Currently we are all divorced or single. Our age is generally the time in life when we start over again. Our first serious relationship is over and we're tired of our jobs and thinking about starting another career. Most of us think our first love will last forever, whether it is a partner or a career. This is the thought process of the youth.

Lexa talks about her ten-year relationship with another woman basketball player. The woman, whose name we cannot say out loud due to the real consequences of homophobia and impact on her fan base, left Lexa after ten years, a joint bank account and a condo on the lake, for male professional basketball player. We can't mention the male basketball player's name because it makes Lexa really angry. Lexa's girlfriend and the male player met at a birthday party that Lexa threw for her. Hopefully her birthday wishes came true as Lexa's wishes did not. Before she left, they were discussing sperm donors for starting a family.

Harley talks about her career as a Naturopath. She is in private practice and enjoying her career. Harley was married until she was forty-five, then woke up one morning and decided she didn't want to be married anymore. It wasn't that she didn't love her husband, she just didn't want to be married. Harley sips her wine as she tells her story. She changes the subject, "Remember when we all got drunk on

Baby Champs and went to Adelina Beach?"

Adelina Beach is the unofficial nudist beach of Baypoint. Being nude in public is actually illegal which increases the thrill of going to a nudist beach. Back in college when we first started going, we enjoyed the feeling of the sun touching all parts of our body. Also, the warmth of the sand, especially after the long, cold winters. Then, the perverts showed up. I should have known, where there are young, pretty women, eventually those who are not so fit as lovers, boyfriends or husbands, will show up. I remember the dawning of this realization. The group of us were laying on the beach with our eyes closed after having a few drinks. Suddenly we became aware of a shadow blocking our sun. The shadow was cast by the body of a naked man who was obviously excited to see us. We all jumped up to get to higher ground, however, we were under the influence of Baby Champs, a very affordable champagne. We were so drunk we couldn't get away. So, Lawren picked up little rocks and threw them at the man's penis.

"Hey, where is Lawren?" "I don't know" I said. "She arrived earlier." I looked around and see Lawren leaning up against the staircase talking to Dr. Walraven. She is laughing and engaged. It appears she got distracted before making it to our table.

Dr. Walraven is a very popular teacher. She teaches Women's Studies and Minority Studies. A very uncommon field for a white woman, though she pulled it off. Emelie, as we often call her, outlasted the criticism that is typical in the field. She is white and privileged. What does she know? The truth is that she was one of the first interested in the subject who was willing and able to teach it. Of course, she was privileged enough to get her Ph.D. and has not experienced racism but she didn't grow up privileged in the traditional sense. When she entered academia no one else in the establishment cared about these issues. This was possibly due to the lack of women and women of color in academia at that time. She was our first exposure to these subjects. Her classes turned my life upside down, in a good way. I could no longer think about the world as I used to. I am grateful for her mentorship.

Dr. Walraven is so easy to talk to and she has quite a following. Emelie is a tall and striking woman. Even in her 70's she is beautiful, with long, flowing whitish-brown hair. Her wrinkles are glowingly attractive. As usual she smiles and makes complete eye contact with Lawren as they talk. Emelie's code of ethics are so highly regarded that many of the faculty, staff and students make decisions based on what they think Emelie would do in a certain situation. Our dinner table was obviously loud enough to distract Lawren from her talk with Emelie. She looks over, excuses herself and heads toward our table. She smiles and yells "This is just like old times."

After dinner, we get more drinks and talk about tomorrow's schedule. The campus has various scholarly talks and activities during reunion weekend. Safehaven's current and former teachers will be in their offices or old lecture rooms. They will be giving lectures and workshops on the latest research in their field. Still others will open up circles so alumni can discuss how education has changed their lives, influenced their careers and encouraged them to give back to their community. What I like about the schedule is that it is reminiscent of being back in college. We wake up in the dorms, eat breakfast in the cafeteria, head off to numerous lectures in various lecture halls, go to the main campus for a barbecue lunch then attend more lectures in the afternoon. Afterwards, we end up in the cafeteria for dinner before heading back to the dorms. A comforting routine of learning, reconnecting and settling in.

There are various interesting lectures and workshops both at Safehaven and on the main campus but we decide to focus primarily on Safehaven College this year, as it is the college's 50th year anniversary. We definitely plan to attend Emilie Walraven's lecture on "Women: 50 years later." However, there are other interesting topics in the schedule, such as Economics and the Environment, Questioning Capitalism, Biology and Epigenetics, Traveling to Other Cultures, Men in Music, Spirituality versus Religion, Biodynamic Farming, Nature Walk on Conundrum Hill, Old Growth Trees at Infinity Lake, Arts in the Safehaven District and an old time favorite, Drumming Circle and Basket Weaving with Natural Fibers. Just to name a few. What I like about basket weaving is that the participants go back and forth between the improv music circle and basket weaving circle. In the end, I am entertained and have made a nice basket to take home with me.

An impressive fact about Safehaven is that many of the teachers joined Safehaven at its' inception and taught until they could no longer manage the long work hours. In many cases, teachers teach into their 70's, often by decreasing their workloads to only one or two classes a day. As a result, Safehaven has many generations of teachers. I think this structure along with its small class size creates a sense of family. Not to say we didn't have subcultures or stratification within our college, as I clearly remember this, like any other social organization. However, I think we were more aware and addressed these issues more consciously than a traditional college.

We finally finish our dinner and drinks. It is approximately 9 pm. We wander back to our dorm rooms. I want to relax and sober up. Harley is rooming with me and Lexa and Juni are rooming together in dorm #11. I follow Harley out on the balcony for a smoke. "What an ironic habit", I comment. Harley replies, "Yeah, I know. I have spent the last twenty-five years smoking and since I am a Naturopath, I have to smoke in the closet, literally. At work, I cannot smoke around anyone, including the staff. All day, I counsel my patients about their need to quit smoking. I picked up the habit during my doctorate program during the long nights studying and even longer days as a resident. At least I smoke the natural type. Organic tobacco with no fillers. We all have our flaws and struggles in life. Don't we?" "Yes" I smile in a supportive way.

"I really want to check on my kids but I can't get any cell service here. I really miss them. It's funny because I never wanted to have children at first. I was too busy with my career and I never met the right person. Then I got an interview for a position with the Department. Once I became a police officer there was no spare time to think about these things. Police training is strenuous, then comes the promotions and with each promotion comes more strenuous training. I just didn't have time and the late nights weren't conducive to family life. As a result of my dedication to my career, I never married. But then, one morning changed my life. I was awakened by an early morning phone call. I was informed that my sister's car was found at the bottom of a high cliff but her body was not recovered. The Department gave me daily updates on the investigation. My Sergeant said the bay below was very deep and cold with strong currents. My sister must have been ejected when her car tumbled down the cliff. She must have been thrown into the bay and caught by the current then forced underwater. He reassured me that she didn't suffer. He was certain she could not have survived the impact of hitting the cliff before reaching the water. He said I didn't have to worry or think about her drowning in the cold, dark, early morning waters. That was the day I became a parent. It was the best and worst thing that ever happened to me. It was a tragedy losing my sister, Johanna. Every day I try to raise Channon and Kaite Lynn the same way their mother would have raised them." Tears roll down my face.

Harley gives me a hug, still holding her cigarette in the one hand. Her filter-less, natural cigarette had burned down, close to her fingers leaving a brownish residue on her fingertips. She carefully puts it out on the balcony railing then places the butt in her pocket. "I like to hide the evidence", she says. I clear my throat, "I think about my sister every day. I miss her so much. It would have been better if we had found her body. Then I could have closure. For years, I held the fantasy that she may still be alive. I am sure it's more like wishful thinking. Maybe she bumped her head and got amnesia. Soon she would remember her family and come knocking on my door. As the years passed, I realized this scenario wasn't likely and I was more able to accept her death. Losing a loved one can really change a person. I will never be the same. I will always have a hole in my heart and a feeling of being incomplete. Every day when I look at Channon and Kaite, I see their mother. Channon has her mother's smile and Kaite has her mother's personality. At least I still see my sister in her children. That is all I have left of her." Harley smiles tenderly. I wipe my eyes and change the subject, "Tomorrow will be a busy day and our night has just begun."

Chapter 2

The Solstice

Lawrence Anderson

It is the evening of June 21st. Coincidentally, every year the reunion falls on the weekend of the Solstice. This is the longest day of sunlight of the year and the transition from Spring to Summer.

As reunion tradition prevails, all four of us meet just before sunset by the pond, outside the dorms between the two brick pathways. One by one we sneak out of the dorm, so we don't draw attention and can meet in secrecy.

We quietly walk toward Safehaven's Biodynamic Farm and the little cabins making up the Sustainable Housing Project. The sun has not yet set and it is still light outside. There is a cool breeze that is refreshing and invigorating. Conundrum Hill sits against the east side

of campus and overlooks the bay and the city of Baypoint.

Thankfully we have sobered up as Conundrum Hill is rough and there is decreased visibility inside the trees at dusk. We alert some of the animals as we pass through the farm. We hear various types of livestock call out, as if they are notifying the other animals of our presence. We pass the chickens, goats, pigs and the cows. We hear a donkey's "hee-haw" drift through the night We start the incline up the hill. I look back to notice all lights are out in the Sustainable Housing, as students are gone for the summer.

Conundrum Hill is a foot-only hill as it is too steep and narrow for cars. It is closed to hikers at dusk because there is no electricity or lighting on the hill. We light some candles to illuminate our way. I lead the pack. It will be about a 25-minute hike to the summit. On several occasions, I hear a distant rustling in the brush but this noise seems at equal distance away from us at all times. I figure it is a nocturnal animal dutifully attending to their business of survival.

I can see the campus below as we gain altitude. It is very quiet at this time of the evening. The hustle and bustle of the day has vanished. The campus is dark with a few exceptional lights along the path that traverses across campus. I look down the other side of the hill and see distant street and business lights of the city. From a distance these lights appear to twinkle. It is a beautiful view. I can smell the moisture settling on the leaves and ground as a slight breeze picks up and flows past us. The same type of smells typical of early morning.

The hill is called Conundrum Hill due to the unusual nature of the hill. It has jagged slabs of rock at different angles that jut out from the landscape. It also has a mystery about it; rumors say it is a meeting ground for a secret society and sacred rituals. Though no one has ever really proved this.

As we reach the top, there is a clearing that is home to a large tree. This tree is a dark and vibrant green. There are no other trees or bushes in the vicinity as if the sandy soil around the tree is hostile toward any other type of vegetation. It is just a single tree that looms toward the heavens. Its' branches reach upward and outward, both vertically and horizontally, filling the sky with its' strong arms. It looks out of place in the rocky, dry, gravel and sand. The students call this tree The Tree of Life because it's iconic structure and age. It is a fruit tree with four different varieties of pears growing on it. This is not so unusual these days but when this tree was planted, several hundreds of years ago, this technology did not exist. Someone must have had an advanced knowledge of trees and grafting at that time. The tree appears quite healthy for its age and, of course, it still bears fruit.

There is a small stream that flows downhill leading to a small pond. This is the main water source for the beautiful tree. Fruit hangs down from the branches. Other branches have blossoms of different colors and fruit in various stages of development.

We sit down under the tree, open our packs and take out more candles. I carefully position four large candles under the tree, facing in each direction, north, south, east and west, representing the four corners of the earth. Harley, Juni and Lexa place smaller candles in between the four larger candles. The larger candles are colored and the smaller candles are white. The large candle facing north is green and symbolizes the Earth. The large candle facing south is red, symbolizing the element of Fire. The large candle facing east is yellow, symbolizing Air and the last large candle facing west is blue, symbolizing Water. We laboriously light all of the candles. The flames flicker and dance, creating a mystical effect. I take out my chalice, some sweet bread, as well as some herbs and incense. The other three take out their chalices. Harley produces several bottles of wine that she smuggled from the cafeteria at dinner. She appears quite proud

Lawrence Anderson

of herself for being able to acquire so much wine without drawing attention to herself.

I think back to how we all met. It was in Dr. Walraven's class, "The Goddess in All of Us", during our freshman year. We were new to the college and had recently left our family, friends and everything familiar to us, to pursue higher education. We started out as awkward and self-conscious but ended the quarter as a confident, tightly knit group. We learned the basics of pagan study. All four of us have since continued to practice what we learned in this class. Dr. Walraven and her class greatly influenced our lives.

We acknowledge the seasons, their importance in nature, the cycles of life, the power of the feminine and the Goddess, as we address the four corners. I pour the wine, filling each chalice. I take my chalice and lift it for a toast. I time the toast for exactly 9:10 pm, as the sun sets. As I get ready to toast, I hear a noise that distracts me. I realize we are not alone. All four of us quickly turn our heads, an automatic reflex, toward the direction of the noise. I see a darting animal that is small with a long, full red tail. It is so quick that I question whether I really saw it or not. I point and asked the others, "Did you see a fox?" They look at me in confusion. I continue to look in the same direction, hoping I can see the animal again to justify my senses. Then I hear a different noise in the same direction. This is a heavier, constant sound, like that of human footsteps. I look back at the others to quickly count them to make sure they are all there. I initially thought Lexa had slipped away to go to the bathroom in the bushes as she often has troubles with her bowels and bladder.

I see a figure emerge from the shadows of the trees and walk toward us. The profile is inconspicuous and the movement stealth, barely audible. It's clear someone has intruded on our gathering. The figure is tall, slender and strong. As the figure gets closer, I examine the dark cloak and hood covering their face. I steady myself for an emergency action, not knowing the intent of this person. A strong voice breaks through the silence, "Shall we toast the Goddess?" A hand appears from the black cloak and pulls back the hood to reveal her face as the sun begins to dip below the horizon.

"Emelie? Dr. Walraven? Is that you?" "Yes, my dear. It is me. I see you're still practicing the craft. I think it's time you learn more about it, including the history of this type of ritual and its association with the university." We all sit speechless as she speaks. We are transfixed by her presence and stare intensely as the last of the sun's rays cross over her face. The sun sets. The candles appear brighter as the atmosphere darkens.

Emelie continues. "I am a witch." Simultaneously, we gasp. "I come from a long line of witches. I am part of a secret society of witches at the university. My parents attended this university, as well my siblings and my grandparents. It is my job, along with the other witches within the coven, to pass along our knowledge and practices. I have been waiting for you to be ready. I believe it's time. Tonight, we celebrate the Solstice. Tomorrow you learn more about our society. Cheers my sister's. To our coven." We all lift our chalices and cautiously take a sip of sweet wine in our shocked state.

We start down Conundrum Hill at approximately midnight. I lead the group with Harley, Juni and Lexa behind me. Dr. Walraven is in the very back. We are quiet, thinking about the night's events. The moon has risen and casts its beams onto our path. As we reach the paved road that separates Conundrum Hill from the campus and signifies the return to civilization, I stop suddenly to ask Emelie a question. As I turn, I notice she is no longer there. I call out to the others in surprise. No one realized she was gone or how long since she disappeared. I look back scanning the trail through the trees to see if I can locate her. There is no movement anywhere. The forest is quiet.

We continue our walk back. The air is stagnant as we walk through the Biodynamic Farm and past the Sustainable Housing Project. There are no sounds from the animals though I can sense they are awake and aware of our presence. Finally, we reach the familiar brick path that leads to the dorms. We sneak into the lower level of Sojourner Truth Hall, the same way we snuck out the night before. This was not the first time I had to sneak back into the dorms early in the morning.

We walk tippy- toe, trying to be quiet and not wake anyone. The lights are out except in the dorm lounge. There is Lawren, sitting quietly on a brown leather upholstered chair, a small lamp highlighting her face. As I walk by, she looks up from her book, "Good night Lawren", I say, surprised but pleased to see her. "Good night", says Lawren, returning to her book.

Lawrence Anderson

Chapter 3

The Tree of Life

Early the next morning I run into Lawren in the shared bathroom between dorms #9 and #10. She is brushing her teeth. I am patting concealer under my eyes. "You were up late last night. Did you have fun?" I avoid her question not knowing what to say. Finally, I reply, "Yes, and I didn't sleep well once I returned to the dorms. A little too much to drink and too much on my mind." "Really" she says. "Um, yeah, we went to The Tree of Life at sunset." "Did you know that tree has four different types of pears on it?" Lawren comments. "No, I didn't", I say looking away. "Did you know the tree is also believed to have special healing powers? Yeah, and the four different varieties of pears represent wisdom, hope, goodness and the power of expression." I reply, "Ah, no, I didn't." "It is also thought to symbolize the four seasons, the four corners of the earth, immortality, the continuation of the generations and the connection between the heaven and earth." "Wow" I say, "You sound like you know a lot about this tree." Lawren smiles coyly, "Urban Legend." I change the subject quickly. "Hey, do you want to go with the group to the lectures today?" Lawren smiles, "Would love to. Hopefully you will be able to stay awake" She laughs. "Meet in Emelie's class at nine?" I say quickly, feeling my face turn red. I abruptly turn around and return to dorm #9, shutting the adjoining bathroom door as I leave.

Harley is making a healthy breakfast. She brought a blender in her suitcase and is blending greens and protein powder. She pours the mixture into a BPA- free smoothie bottle and tightens the lid. "This is for the road", she says. She reaches out the window and grabs a burning cigarette that is resting on the windowsill. She inhales deeply and appears relieved. She exhales out the window and waves away the residual smoke from inside the room.

Juni and Lexa are already waiting in the dorm lounge and looking over the day's schedule. Harley quickly tosses a mint in her mouth as we walk, to cover up her cigarette breath. I tell the others about the strange conversation I had with Lawren in the bathroom earlier. I also tell them about how she blurted out all these facts about The Tree of Life and how I invited her to hang out with us due to my discomfort with the conversation. They just looked at me as if I'm crazy.

We head off toward the cafeteria. Today the cafeteria is honoring Safehaven's Biodynamic Farm by using produce from the farm for all three meals. The breakfast menu lists organic, scrambled, free range chicken eggs, organic potatoes and organic carrot juice. I always look forward to Saturday because it's not the typical cafeteria food. The Biodynamic Farm grows a variety of food and it is sustainable by itself. All animal feed comes from the fields and garden. Then the wastes from the animals go back to the garden and fields in the form of fertilizer or compost making the farm self- contained and self-sufficient. The farm also has a vineyard and a wine program. I am especially looking forward to tasting the wine tonight. We have nicknamed the Biodynamic Farm, the "pharm" for short. This is the combination of the word's pharmacy and farm since the farm is known for its large variety of medicinal herbs and plants.

I sit quietly with my eyes closed as I savor each bite of breakfast. Saturdays are a sensual experience because of my appreciation for fresh, local and homemade food. I notice the color of the egg yolks. They are bright orange and have a soft, smooth texture as I bite into them. The potatoes are fingerlings that have a deep purple or light red colored flesh. They are dense and creamy. Just the way I like them. They taste even better with fresh sautéed garlic. The carrot juice is frothy and comforting as it goes down.

I look at the time. "Hey guys, it's 8:55. We are going to be late for Emelie's lecture on "Women 50 years later." Harley quickly pours out her green smoothie from her BPA-free bottle into a nearby garbage can. She replaces it with fresh carrot juice. She does not realize she has an orange mustache from the carrot juice.

Juni reaches over and forks a fingerling potato off of Lexa's plate. Lexa makes a sad face and pulls her plate back, out of Juni's reach.

Juni dips the fingerling into a small white, paper condiment cup full of ketchup. Lexa jeers at Juni. The three of us leave Juni at the table with a half-eaten fingerling sticking out her mouth. Juni shoves the rest of the potato in her mouth and runs to catch the group.

We run up the stairs to Safehaven College and settle into Emelie Walraven's classroom. Lawren is already there. When she sees me, she smiles and moves to an unoccupied chair next to me. The chairs are still in the same circle formation they were when we were students. We sit in the same chairs we sat in our freshman year. Harley is on the other side of me and Lexa and Juni are sitting next to her. Emelie is standing while everyone else in the room is sitting.

She appears distracted and less attuned to her students as usual. Her clothing is long, flowing and made out of natural fibers, as usual. Her face is tense. She welcomes everyone but her greeting is shorter than usual. Emelie has always been good with names. She remembers all of her student's names, even decades later. She addresses everyone by their first name and makes an accurate reference to something particular about each person.

Her affect changes as she starts her lecture. She begins her talk on the status of women over the last 50 years. She talks about women and minority women's wages as an indicator of their status in society. Emelie cites, "Women in 1966 earned 57.6 % of what an average man earned. In 2013 women's wages increased to 78.3% of what men made. Therefore, women earned roughly $25,000 a year in the mid 1960's, whereas men earned roughly $42,000 per year. In 2010 women earned roughly $39,000 to men's $51,000.

Emelie pauses in a distracted manner. She losses her train of thought for a moment. This is very unusual, as Dr. Walraven has excellent public speaking skills. I follow Emelie's line of vision, over my shoulder, to a man briefly standing outside the door of the classroom. He was staring at Emelie then quickly disappeared. Emelie looks concerned then shakes her head slightly "Where was I?" Our group sends glances at each other.

Lawren did not appear to notice anything unusual. Emelie continues. "There is a larger gap when you look at minority women in comparison to white men. In 2014 Hispanic women made 54%, Native American women 57%, African American women 63% and white women 78% percent of what white men earned respectively. One exception seems to be Asian women who earned considerably more than the average woman but still less than white men, at 90%."

Emelie purposes possible reasons to explain the gap in earnings and how this gap is less significant if a woman goes into business for herself. Emelie discusses women's role in society and sums up her lecture by suggesting what we can do to make wages more equitable. She finishes ten minutes early and leaves the room abruptly. Before she leaves, she bends over and whispers in my ear. "Meet me at the pharm's herb garden tonight at 10:00 pm."

The four of us gather in the hallway after the lecture. I try to hide my feelings of concern. I comment, "Emelie seemed out of sorts. She wants to meet at the herb garden tonight." Just then, Lawren joins the circle "What did you say about a meeting tonight?" I stammer, "Oh", I say, "We are meeting tonight at Safehaven lounge to watch the band called Herb Garden." "Yeah", Lexa butts in, "They play organic folk music with a medicinal feel. Uh, umm, they play here perennially. I've seen them before and I like them very mulch." Lexa eyes are wide as she tries to cover up our true plans for this evening. "Okay" Lawren says, directing her eyes to the side of Lexa and wrinkling her face. She is not sure how to take Lexa's comments.

We leave Safehaven College taking the steps down to the brick pathway leading toward main campus. Lawren is in tow and therefore, we have to be careful what we say. Our next lecture is at Helen Hall which is located in the middle of campus on the left-hand side of the brick pathway. Helen is the business college. I am distracted because I am still thinking of Emelie and our meeting tonight.

The lecture topic is Economics and the Environment by Professor Swhart. I'm interested in hearing about his research. The lecture hall is in the basement of Helen which is one of the older buildings on campus. We arrange ourselves in a single file as we step down the narrow staircase that leads to the lecture hall below. The air becomes cooler and more stagnant as we descend to the theater type seating below. The floor is concrete and the chairs are made of wood and metal. They are the type of chairs that fold up when not being used.

The five of us take the first five seats in the middle isle, in front of the podium. Simultaneously, we push our seats to the down position and they squeak in symphony. The sound echoes throughout the hall. The audience is small for this lecture. The professor is not yet in the lecture hall. I don't know Professor Swhart.

We were all Safehaven students and therefore, spent most of our time down at the liberal arts side of campus. I did take some

economics classes at Safehaven but there is a difference between traditional business courses at the main campus and economics at Safehaven College. Safehaven tends to look at economics in a holistic manner and considers the social implications of our economic system, such as who it benefits, what are the ethical and environmental issues and so forth. I held hope that someone at the main campus business college, possibly Professor Swhart, could speak about the enlightened side of business, not just the bottom line. I have heard some good reviews of the professors at Helen Hall. Obviously, Professor Swhart was concerned about the environment based on the title of his lecture.

It is now 10:05 am and still no Professor Swhart. We start to get restless. Just then a thin stream of light reaches out into the rows of wooden seats. This effect is caused by a door opening at the lower level of the hall, near the podium. A room, behind a door that was better lit than the lecture hall. I notice a human shadow slowly emerge. I could not see a face as the light comes from behind. The figure is rigid and slightly hunched over. His gait is slow and restricted in movement. He limps into the spotlight that lights the podium.

Professor Swhart is a short statured man with jet black hair, except for approximately a quarter inch of strands on either side of his part. These strands are pure white. This contrast gives him an unusual and unsettling appearance. He stands at the podium for a minute without saying a word. Then he lets out a cackling cough. The type of cough that sounds wet and heavy. He wipes his mouth with his sleeve then introduces himself in a crackly voice. "I am Dr. Swhart. I am a tenured professor and researcher at Helen Hall. My current research is looking at Fortune 500 businesses and assigning an objective rating system to each business. These ratings weigh the businesses' positive impact on the economy versus its environmental impact. For example, let's look at the practice of fracking natural gas from the earth. Here, I would objectively rate a business, such as the corporation named Fossil Frack Corp, based on its contribution to the economy. I give it a number between 1 and 100, then I objectively rate this corporation's negative impact on the environment. I subtract the second number from the first number to get a number representing an overall score. Therefore, Fossil Frack Corp has greatly impacted the economy of many small towns in a positive manner. I rate this company's economic impact at 99. Then I look at the environmental impact this corporation has on the water, wildlife and the health of the community. The objective number for this corporation's negative environmental impact is 25. I subtract 25 from 99 and the overall rating is 74. Since this is a positive number and it is close to 100, this company is rated above average for its positive impact on the community. This rating positively affects the corporation rating on the Stock Exchange."

Professor Swhart continues by talking in depth about the business profile of Fossil Frack Corp, including its profits and dividends to its stockholders. He finishes his lecture by introducing his graduate students who are helping him on the project. Professor Swhart announces "Alan, Nefara and Odious." There is a faint sound of clapping from the back of the lecture hall. One by one, all three of the graduate students walk out from the darkness into the spot light. As the third grad student emerges, I recognize his face. Odious is tall, thin and pale. He is wearing straight, tight legged, dark denim jeans. He smiles slightly and nods as he looks into the audience. On his nose sits square, black rimmed glasses that reflects the spotlight back to the audience. He is physically but not emotionally present. I can't tell if this is a personality trait or a characteristic of an arrogant graduate student. As quickly as he appears in the spotlight, he steps back into the darkness just outside the reach of the light.

There is a loud noise overhead as all of the lights in the lecture hall shut off. The effect is similar to the old days when someone took a picture with a light cube. It left you temporarily blind. As my vision comes back, Professor Swhart and his colleagues have disappeared from the stage. Harley announces. "That was not what I expected." I add, "Me neither." Harley adds sarcastically in a funny voice, "I am going to call my stockbroker to buy Fossil Frack stocks." Juni pipes in, "Yeah, we can recruit a small town under economic stress and sign them up with Fossil Frack, after all it has a 74 rating." Lexa comments, "I think Swhart is a fwart, get it.? His economics stink", she giggles.

It was 11:00 am and we decided to skip the Picnic on Old Main lawn to go to the Spirits and Hors d' Oeuvres in the Library. The Old Library is inside the building called Old Main. Wasgard University's old campus is at the opposite end of the campus from Safehaven College. Old Main is over a hundred years old. Wasgard was originally a private Normal School, meaning it was a school to teach teachers. In 1893 it became a public college named Newcome Normal School.

This was long before the college of Safehaven was established in the mid 1960's.

It is a partly sunny or partly cloudy day. Some of the clouds are white and billowy, while other clouds are dark and heavy. I hope it doesn't rain. We slowly walk and talk from Helen Hall through Red Square toward the Old Main lawn. Old Main is north of Red Square. There are old growth evergreen trees and a selection of rare deciduous trees that line the red brick walkway that lead students from the north end of the main campus to Red Square. Red Square is a focal point of the old campus. It is called Red Square due to the expansive red brickwork. It is a common meeting point for students between classes. In the very center of the brickwork is a large granite fountain. Many of the northern buildings and colleges face Red Square and the fountain. One of these building is the newer Library.

During my college years, religious groups gathered at the fountain in Red Square, singing religious songs and "ministering" to the students. This was the era of Ronald Reagan and the Religious Right. Students were more religiously active than politically active back then, except for Safehaven College.

The old stone building called Old Main stands in the distance as one looks up from the lawn area where the picnic is being held. Old Main is elevated from the rest of the campus. The details of the building speaks to how old it is. The materials used and the detail are telltale of its era. It's obvious that the builders took great pride in their craft.

There weren't many people gathered on the lawn for the picnic. Maybe they changed their minds, as we did, and decided to engage in lighter fare inside the Old Library. We climb a long flight of granite stairs that lead to the stone building. Just as I reach for the door handle of the heavy institutional door to Old Main, I feel raindrops pelt me in the back of the head. I pull the door forcibly hurrying to get into the building before I get any wetter. The air in the building smells musty. Dampness lays in the air. We have to go up another internal flight of stone stairs before reaching the former library. The Old Library is finished in marble and wood and the walls are covered with old, wood shelving that starts at the floor and continues up the walls to the vaulted ceilings. Old antiquated books remain on the shelves. There are old paintings lining the walls and large wool rugs with fine detail covering the spacious floors.

A group of young students are on top of a make-shift stage

getting ready to play for the returning alumni. They are playing different scales and tuning their instruments. People are funneling in through doors on either side of the library. We have to walk in line as people quickly fill the room. Harley grabs the back of my shirt and holds on so she doesn't get lost in the crowd. The crowd varies significantly from professors and older alumni to young students, prospective students and their parents. I stop abruptly causing Harley to run into the back of me. I am captivated by a large painting on the wall. It is a portrait of an aristocratic looking woman. She has long, full and flowing blondish hair, high cheek bones and a noble nose. A brass name plate below the painting identifies her as Lady Madsen. Her portrait hangs in the hub of the Normal School library to acknowledge her dedication and contribution to the profession of teaching.

The band finally starts playing in unison. There is a mixture of classical and modern instruments giving the resulting music a hybrid quality. I think to myself how the younger generation of students are not afraid to be creative or bold. This is a refreshing quality of the youth. I seize an empty table that the group can stand around. It is a tall bistro table that is made to stand around rather than sit at. It has a black iron frame and white tile tabletop. Most tables are already occupied. Harley, Lexa, Juni and finally Lawren encircle the table. A current student, working the reunion for extra spending money, approaches the table. He is holding a serving tray with drinks and Hors d' Oeuvres. Each of us take a glass of wine and a rice Dolma off the tray.

I offer a toast, "To the reunion, good friends, good food, good wine and getting out of the rain." I raise my flute high into the circle.

Harley, Lexa, Juni and Lawren raise their flutes and repeat my toast. We drink in the flavor of the Northwest wine. It is fruity, slightly bubbly and refreshing. Lexa misses her lips and spills the wine down the front of her white shirt leaving a long, red stain.

The music shifts to a faster beat leading to a crescendo. A movement in the crowd catches my eye. I see a person quickly open a door to the side of the library and pass through its threshold. The door closes as quickly as it opened. I recognize this person as being one of the graduate students from our previous lecture. It is the same person I briefly saw in the doorway at Safehaven during Dr. Walraven's lecture. I think to myself how quickly he was able to make his rounds through campus. I wonder what it is about this young man that disturbed Emelie. He does look suspicious. I wonder what he is doing and where that door leads.

The Spirits and Hors d' Oeuvres in the Library was winding down and the afternoon lectures were about to begin. We are scheduled for the Nature Walk on Conundrum Hill. I convince the others to leave without me and I would catch up with them later. I tell them the wine has gone to my head and I want sit and drink coffee for a while. Harley wants to rub my meridians to sober me up but I convince her to go on without me. She seems disappointed but reluctantly runs off to catch the others.

The library is almost empty except for a few student employees who are cleaning up. Luckily, I am wearing a white shirt and black pants today. My wardrobe looks similar to the uniform of the hired staff. I grab a serving tray and start picking up dirty plates and wine glasses. This way I won't be shooed out of the library with the rest of the guests. I wipe down a table near the door that the grad student disappeared through.

The student employees work at a high rate of speed around me. They don't seem to notice anything unusual about me. I hear two of them talking about a concert on campus later tonight. They are so excited to go. "It is an impromptu performance by an anonymous female performer. It's not even on the schedule of events. It is rumored this performer was on tour in Canada and the university convinced her to cross the border after her scheduled concerts." That would certainly explain the bus and entourage I saw earlier today on campus. The bus was painted with rainbow colors and looked like a throwback to the 1960's.

The students rush off to get good seats on the outdoor plaza. They will be sitting there for hours before the concert starts but will be close to the stage. I am envious but have other important things to do, such as find out where that door leads.

I wait for all of the employees to leave before I approach the old wooden door. The molding around the door is elaborately detailed like the other wood and stonework throughout the building. There is a carved centerpiece above the door. To the side of the detailed frame is a security keypad that has numbers on it. Without a code, I can't get through the door. I grasp the brass doorknob and push on the door. To my surprise, it opens. I realize that the wood door is old and swollen with age which prevents it from shutting tight enough to engage the lock. The door moves past its sticking point. The hinges are rusty and give resistance.

The threshold leads to a hallway that is long and dark. There is stonework that looks much older than the detail in the library. There is a pattern in the stonework that repeats itself using different sized stones, setting this work apart from the Old Main stonework. The lighting is poor and it appears this area was originally lit by candles via candle chandeliers and sconces. The hallway leads to a large area that opens up, revealing old wooden shelves and wooden drawers that compartmentalize the area into smaller spaces. This is probably the original library of Old Main. There are old books and artifacts stored on the shelves. The drawers have skeleton keyholes. I see stacks of old books and scrolls with painted portraits of people dressed in ancient styles of clothing. I do not understand the writing on the book that is sitting on top of the stack. The characters are unfamiliar. I continue to explore by walking to the end of a hall leading away from the library into a distant room. I look up to see a vast stained-glass section in the ceiling. It is a pastel purple color. It was probably used to light the room with natural light in the days when there was no electricity available. The design is a large mandala with a majestic tree inside. The stained glass shows the trees extending branches and large root system.

I walk under the large plate of glass and look up to examine the fine detail and symbols in the glass. The light coming down from the sun outside highlights the glass. It casts a purple hue causing my skin and clothing to turn a light shade of purple. I stand underneath its faint light with my hands raised in astonishment. I am speechless as I experience its ambiance. I am awakened from my amazement by proximate voices. They sound close but muffled. It sounds like a group of people. I stand frozen, listening. Then, I recognize the voices. It is Harley, Lexa, Juni and Lawren talking to each other about The Tree of Life. For a minute, I am confused but then I realize the voices are coming from outside, on the other side of the stained glass. How can that be? Is it the group from the Nature Walk on Conundrum Hill that I hear above? My attention is diverted by the sounds of footsteps nearby. I turn and run as fast as I can, hoping I won't be detected. I exit the sticking door leading back into the library where we just had Spirits and Hors d' Oeuvres.

I run across the library and exit down the stone steps, trying to dart out of sight. Once I gain some distance, I criticize myself. Obviously, I saw Odious enter but not exit the area. He was always back there the whole time I was there. What was I thinking? My heart beats faster at this thought.

I run down the outdoor granite staircase and through Red Square. I head toward Conundrum Hill in such a panic that I run off the brick walkway and bushwhack through the trees. I stumble on uneven ground, twist my ankle, fall and tumble in the brush. I pick up sticks, leaves and dirt on my hands, knees and in my hair from the rough landing. I scurry to get back on my feet.

The group sees me. Harley looks concerned, "You are sweaty and flushed. Are you okay?" She places her hand on my forehead before reaching up to remove a small stick from my hair. I tell her that sometimes I have an allergic reaction to the sulfites in wine. This is a lie, of course, but I couldn't go into detail at this time. She looks puzzled and reminds me that she has seen me drink plenty of wine before without a reaction. She puts two fingers to my Carotid Artery and announces "Your heart rate is high." I tell her "No, don't worry, I will be fine. I'll just keep walking." She watches me as I pace to get my heart rate down. My body is amped from the rush of adrenaline that I need to burn off. Sweat runs down my forehead.

I ask her "How is the nature walk?" Harley hesitates before replying. "We learned a little about the history of the hill but the story about The Tree of Life is contrary to what we know. The professor said that it was planted forty years ago, by an organization called The Drothers. Where did he get his history? Clearly this tree is older than that and what about Emily and Edward's version of the story?" I look through Harley and reply. "Nothing is as it seems. There seems to be more mystery on this campus than one could imagine." I think of the Ancient Library and Odious.

The group decides to attend the lecture on Biodynamic Farming. We meet at the pharm's Learning Center. This is where Safehaven College teaches classes in horticulture, agriculture, permaculture, viticulture and oenology. In other words, sustainable farming, livestock, tending of grapevines and the making of wine.

The Center is an old barn like structure with walls on only three sides. It is an outdoor classroom. The siding is made of reclaimed lumber and is very weathered. The floor of the classroom is carpeted with loose hay atop a dirt floor. The chairs are bales of hay or log rounds to sit on. There is a fire pit in the center.

We sit in a circle which is usual for Safehaven. The classroom opens up to the fields on the side of the structure where the missing fourth wall would be. It reminds me of the old barn I used to play in at my aunt and uncle's farm when I was young. The smell of the hay brings back this pleasant memory. I breathe in the earthy smell and feel the warmth of its insulating effects. There is a breeze coming through the open side of the structure that is refreshing. It is amazingly cozy and rejuvenating which is surprising considering my day.

An older man standing near the fire introduces himself. He states he is the caretaker of the Biodynamic Farm. I estimate him to be in his 60's but it is hard to tell. He is a small framed man with a full head of silvery brown-blonde hair. It is obvious he was quite handsome in his youth, although he is still very handsome. I notice that even though he works with his hands, they are clean, soft and youthful.

Edward's manner is somewhat timid and shy but he is clearly a compassionate and honorable man. He seems uncomfortable talking about himself, unlike some professors I have known. He tells the group that he has been working on the farm since the inception of Safehaven College. He describes biodynamic farming as a holistic approach to agriculture. He talks about sustainability and how wastes are converted back to useful materials within the farm. He talks about how biodynamic farming practices believe in treating the animals ethically. Edward describes the philosophy based on Rudolf

Lawrence Anderson

Steiner's concepts. His light blue eyes sparkle and pierce his audience as he speaks. He makes witty jokes that make us laugh. Edward leads the group on a tour to include the animals, the compost piles where he uses the animal wastes to make fertilizer, the vineyards and the herb garden which he appears to be especially proud of. He uncharacteristically boasts that he has the largest collection of herbs on the west coast. Edward bends down and breaks off a handful of green pointed leaves. He gives each one of us a leaf to chew on. I smell it before putting it in my mouth and biting down on it. "Aw, peppermint", I say to myself.

I gently chew the peppermint as I look out across the pharm to see several types of animals running freely through the fields. I absentmindedly continue to scan the area for additional roaming livestock but instead I see a young woman walking across my line of vision. She catches my eye. She is walking on the trail from the main campus toward the district of Safehaven. I think to myself and it suddenly hits me. I spit out the peppermint leaf and gasp.

She is Nefara, one of the triad graduate students from the Business College under Dr. Swhart. I fix on her, following her progression down the trail. She is wearing a long silky, loose knitted shirt similar to a Henley. It comes to a V below her chest, showing her cleavage. Her thin, strait black hair falls onto her exposed chest. She flips her head causing her hair to shuffle between her natural color and her blonde highlights. Her olive skin appears to absorb the warmth of the sun. Several steps behind her is a man. I stop breathing and sit motionless as he comes into the center of my vision. Odious walks fast to catch up with her. Neither one of them look our way as they walk by. I sink down, making myself smaller. I would have disappeared if I could. I watch until they fade out of sight. I think what an odd combination.

Edward finishes his talk. He announces that the pharm needs volunteers and points to a sign-up sheet on a clipboard hanging on the wall of the Learning Center. The group claps in gratitude. As I applaud, I observe a pygmy goat come up from behind Edward. The short, fat, spotted goat uses his head to ram Edward. The goat stands straight up on his hind legs then curls his head and butts forward hitting Edward's backside. Although very cute and funny, we are unsure how to react to this display. It becomes clear by the goat's delight that this is a gesture of affection, not aggression. Edward smiles and reaches back with his hand to rub the goat's head. The goat bleats making a high pitch sound like a drunken teenager. The group circles around Edward and the goat to ask questions. I want to ask a question but there are too many people around him.

Harley leans against me. She is impressed by Edwards's collection of medicinal plants. "I wish I had his pharmacy. I could treat thousands of people with this quantity of plants." I interject, "I am sure he is the envy of all Naturopaths." Harley jokes, "I wonder if he has any ganja hidden in these fields." We smile at each other in a knowing way. After all, it is Safehaven College. Marijuana is our unofficial mascot.

It is late afternoon and the lectures and workshops are finished for the day. Lexa comes to remind me that Basket Weaving with Natural Fibers is Sunday morning and we will have to make our annual appearance. I reassure her that I would not miss it for the life of me. Even though, I already have numerous, unusual looking woven baskets sitting around my house in Cedar Crest.

Lawren asks the four of us what we are doing later this evening. She says she heard there is a last-minute concert scheduled and the surprise performer is an accomplished musician. Juni yawns loudly, "I can't make it. I am pretty tired." Harley coughs unconvincingly, "I am not feeling well." Lawren turns to me. Not knowing what to say, I say, "Gee I'm really sorry but I already have a date tonight." Lawren appears bewildered looking at Lexa, as she is the last person in the group to ask. Lexa, stutters and blurts out, "I am volunteering....at the Biodynamic Farm...to clean the barn...yeah, I love feces from different species." Just then Edward walks by, hears this and thanks Lexa for her community service. She smiles awkwardly and says with faded enthusiasm "It's a shitty job but someone has to do it." Lawren looks rejected and turns away. I feel bad but the group is supposed to meet Emily tonight and Lawren cannot know this. Besides Lexa and I only made a half-lie, as I do have a date with Emily and Lexa will be at the pharm tonight.

Chapter 4

Hanging in the Balance

For some reason, I have a very large appetite. It is either due to all of the excitement of the day or because Saturday is the day the cafeteria serves my favorite meals at the reunion. Like breakfast, dinner is prepared from food grown at the Biodynamic Farm, including the wine. The menu is a surprise and based on whatever is available from the pharm that day. We meet at the usual place, the table we always sit at. As a group, we walk together and stand in the food line. I am eager and can't wait to see what is for dinner. I step in front of Harley and she tries to step back in front of me but I hold her back. I grab a tray. Lexa also steps in front of Harley using an old basketball move called "blocking out." This move in basketball blocks an opponent from getting to the basket or from making a defensive move. It is very effective and stops the others from getting in front of me, as well.

Dinner is fava beans and quinoa in herb sauce, spicy corn on the cob, coleslaw with carrots, yellow fingerling potatoes, berry salad, frozen dessert and Pinot Noir wine. After we get our food and sit down, I grab my fork with passion, anticipating every bite. Edward's signature is all over this meal. The fava beans have pieces of crisp asparagus flavored with garlic, mint, parsley, scallions and hazelnuts. The quinoa is soft and nutty. The corn on the cob has multicolored kernels and is seasoned with coriander, chili powder and a dash of cumin. The coleslaw is made with beautiful tender, purple cabbage and shredded carrots, flavored with onions and mustard in a wine vinegar. The fingerling potatoes are yellow, firm and melt in my mouth. The berry salad is made with strawberries, blueberries, raspberries, blackberries, mint and a touch of honey. Lastly, the dessert is organic ice cream or frozen almond dessert. It is hard to believe all of these ingredients are directly from the Biodynamic Farm.

After savoring every bite, I wash it all down with a delectable Pinot Noir that has notes of black raspberry, vanilla, citrus and caramel. Harley laughs. "You were so focused on the food that I chanted Earth to Andi, Come-in Andi, but you didn't hear me." I turn a Pinot shade of red. I quickly make a toast to the Biodynamic Farm, especially the vineyards.

Lawren is distant at dinner and leaves quickly after eating. I didn't see her in the connecting bathroom of the dorm. She didn't brush her teeth after eating, as usual. I hate to hurt her but I really need her to be out of the way tonight. I am sure she feels unwanted after our rejections earlier. Hopefully I can mend our friendship later.

Harley has again smuggled wine from the cafeteria. I bring out my organic Zinfandel. I pull the corks and empty the bottle of pharm wine first, pouring equal amounts into each plastic cup. Disposable red, plastic cups are the official cups of the campus. "Don't these cups bring back memories?" Juni groans, "Yeah, they remind me of horrific hangovers." Lexa brags, "I was a beer pong champion." She gestures like she is throwing a ping pong ball into Juni's cup. I comment, "I knew there was a reason I switched from beer to a drinking wine." Harley reminds everyone that she was too stoned to get hangovers in college. We toast. It seems funny that everything tastes good in these cups.

I wanted to give the girls an update on the events earlier in the day before meeting with Emily tonight. Feeling nervous, I decide to move our meeting into the laundry room, so we will not have to explain ourselves should Lawren come back to the dorm room. "No one will overhear us here." It is hot and there are no windows to open to decrease the humidity which has built up in the room. There is a dryer going, making it hard to hear. I smell the strong scent of dryer sheets that is distracting and changes the taste of the wine we are drinking.

The group is gathered in a circle. I lower my voice, "Remember when I said I had too much wine in the library today?" The others look intently at me and say "yeah." I continue "I know this is a shock, but I lied." I told them about seeing Odious enter a code and go through a door leading into the Ancient Library. Lexa interrupts,

"Who is Odious?" Juni encourages me to continue. "Well, the door didn't close completely, so I was able to open it without a code. It led to an older library which was probably the original library for the university. It had all these antiquated books and things. There were scrolls with funny symbols and in a back room was a stained-glass reproduction of The Tree of Life in the ceiling. As I stood there admiring the glass, I heard you guys talking." I quote the conversation they were having verbatim. Their eyes widened as they listen. "The stained-glass is actually under the pond that is beside The Tree of Life on Conundrum Hill."

It was close to the time we were supposed to meet Emelie at the Biodynamic Farm. The dryer made a long, piercing noise indicating the drying cycle was over. I jump due to feeling nervous someone may discover our covert meeting. I end the meeting and push the others outside. I am glad to leave the noise, the heat and the smell of the dryer sheets. The fresh air and cooler temperature feels good. I look up at the sky. It's getting dark but the sky is holding on to the last glimmer of sunlight. I look toward the pharm. I am looking forward to seeing Emelie.

As we walk toward the pharm, I notice the moon is almost full except for a small sliver. The dirt on the trail is dry and collapses under my feet as I step down. In the distance, I hear the rustling of brush. I wonder if this is Emelie coming from the other direction. The rustling becomes more distant rather than closer. Then I hear gekkering.

The pharm animals are quiet except for an occasional bleat of a goat, whinny of a horse, cluck of a chicken or moo of a cow. The moon lights up the herb garden that carpets the clearing behind the dorms. Emelie suddenly appears out of nowhere. She looks beautiful with the moon behind her. Edward follows her. The two seem unusually comfortable with one another. They make a pretty pair.

Emelie introduces Edward not knowing we attended his lecture and tour of the pharm earlier. I inform her that I am a fan of his harvest. He smiles humbly. It's obvious that she confides in and respects him. She announces that we may speak freely in Edward's presence.

Emelie's manner changes abruptly to business. "Girls lately I have become aware of a growing imbalance on campus. This imbalance is between the good and evil forces. This campus and Conundrum Hill are sacred to us. These have been our meeting grounds and the home to The Tree of Life. People like us have worshiped here freely, even before the campus was built. Many of our ancestors who worshiped here were able to join the university after the campus was built, as many were highly educated. We lived in harmony until about thirty years ago. This is when our coven began to have fundamental differences. Some in the coven wanted to dabble in gray or dark magic. They said it was for a greater good. This magic would increase our powers to do good in the world. But the elders could not justify this means to an end. They were against using dark magic under any circumstance and were conscious of how the use of this type of magic could alter the forces in the world. In the end, the coven split. Many relationships were severed. Families and friendships split. It caused distrust, resentment and a basis for retaliation. The witches that abandoned our group developed their own philosophies and values that did not align with our basic tenets. Instead of using only white magic they integrated gray and dark magic as well. Eventually they transitioned to dark magic completely. This was for several reasons. Dark magic is quicker, easier and initially more powerful. The practice of dark magic does not have moral values. Therefore, if you want to use dark magic for personal gain, this is considered acceptable, whereas, this practice would be completely unacceptable in our coven. Over the years, the dark witches gained wealth and power on campus and in the community. Until recently we were able to balance the dark magic with our use of white magic."

Emelie pauses and in her silence, the crickets in the background become louder, almost deafening. We stand wide-eyed, distracted by the crickets but unable to break eye contact with Emelie. Edward nods in agreement breaking our captivation.

Emelie resumes, "Our coven is aware of you girls. We have been watching you. We are aware that you have been celebrating the Solstice and practicing some of the beliefs, traditions and rituals of our coven since taking my class, The Goddess in All of Us, some thirty years ago. Unfortunately, our coven has been lackadaisical but growing concerns have prompted us to pay more attention and seek new members. This is why we are here tonight to induct you into our coven and ask you to join our forces, for the good. As your mentor, I welcome you."

Emelie continues. "Edward is our herbalist and a trusted member of the coven. He and other trusted coven's members are here to assist you, including myself. In our coven, a woman's power strengthens at the dawning of menopause and continues to gain strength as our life force is redirected from the energy used for reproduction. Our power also gains strength around the Solstice, as well. You have both these events working in your favor at this time. The reverse is true for the dark witches. They are stronger when they are younger.

Anyhow, the dark forces have discovered the code to get into the Ancient Library which is the repository of our archives, artifacts and place of ceremony. Our history, tradition and future are compromised. Thus, the balance between good and evil is in jeopardy. We are afraid that our culture will fall as many others in history have. Those who conquer, destroy the history and culture of those they conquer. We must not let this happen. This is an unsettling time for our kind."

"Just before midnight tonight I will initiate all of you into our coven. Let's meet at Old Main, thirty minutes before midnight. Here are four robes. Please return to your rooms to rest. Remember no food or drink." Emelie and Edward turn and disappear into the darkness. I can't hear the sound of their footsteps in the distance. The woods are quiet.

I turn to Harley, Juni and Lexa with my mouth wide open. Harley says, "I have only dressed up as a witch for Halloween." Lexa says, "I can't wait to get my broom." Juni laughs in a high-pitched voice. She stops herself, putting her finger to her lower lip. In surprise, she says, "That just sounded like a witch's cackle." We look at the robes. There is a purple, red, blue and yellow robe. Juni claims the red robe." The other two grab the blue and yellow robes. I take the remaining purple robe.

Chapter 5

Rebirth

After returning to the dorm, I set the alarm on my cell phone to wake me at 11:00 pm. I lie down but can't sleep. My mind keeps going over the day's events. I think about the large portrait in the library and the unusual symbols in the Ancient Library. These all seem vaguely and strangely familiar. I hear Harley softly snoring. I drift off for what seems like a few seconds but am abruptly awakened by the sound of my alarm. The music of Fleetwood Mac's Rhiannon plays. "Rhiannon rings like a bell through the night. And wouldn't you love to love her? Takes through the sky like a bird in flight. And who will be her lover? All your life you've never seen a woman taken by the wind. Would you stay if she promised you heaven? Will you ever win? She is like a cat in the dark. And then she is the darkness.... Rhiannon." As soon as I realize the theme of the song, I quickly hit my snooze button. I lay stiff in my bed, staring at the ceiling with my heart pounding. It is quiet again. Abruptly, Harley's alarm blares. It is a song written by the rock group Heart called The Witch. "...She's got long black hair. And a big black car. I know what you're thinkin'. But you won't get far. She's gonna make you itch. Cuz she's a witch."

We both sit straight up in bed, staring at each other. Simultaneously, we let out a scream, jump out of bed and turn on the lights as fast as we can. Harley stands on top of her bed then starts jumping up and down, bouncing on her mattress. She announces, "I don't want to go out there. It is dark and almost midnight." I remind her that we will be in the safe hands of Emelie.

I shower, dry off then grab my purple robe. I sit quietly as Harley showers. She exits the shower and grabs her yellow robe. We meet

Juni and Lexa in the student lounge. They are in their robes. Luckily, it is late and there is no one walking across campus. Our dress could draw attention. There is a southern wind blowing against our backs. The robes blow out in front of us. I reach out to grab the flapping fabric, afraid I may lose it in the wind. It is odd to get such a strong wind this time of the year. We reach Red Square and head toward Old Main. Emelie is not waiting at the top of the stairs. We lean against the banister and look out over the Old Main lawn. I can see bats darting in and out of the radius of light that is cast by the lamp below. There is a faint sound of a band playing across campus. I recognize the rhythm of the song but cannot hear the words. The fans are applauding and cheering loudly with enthusiasm.

Emelie is already inside and opens the heavy door to let us in. She is dressed in her celebratory garb. Her robe is also purple but is made from a dark velvet material. She has some sort of head dressing on. It is sparkling and brilliant. She greets us and takes us up the internal stairs into the library. The portraits on the walls of the library are haunting in the dark. We head for the side door, the door Odious went through. Emelie punches in the code 122112. The door beeps. Emelie pushes hard on it and it opens. "I need to change that code and have Edward fix this door."

As we walk past the shelves, I see the scrolls and point them out, so the others can witness the strange symbols. In the distance, there is a glow of candles coming from the room with the stained-glass and people are waiting inside. There is an amazing display of robes. All different colors, designs, art work and stitching. Many robes have similar symbols on them but many appear to be customized to express the individual witch's interests and abilities. All the robed witches have their faces covered with veils. Some of the veils are fine and sheer, while other veils are heavy, loosely weaved or made of tapestry. These veils conceal the witch's identity. Some veils are resting down on the face, exposing their eyes in an intriguing manner, while others wear their veils so that their face is covered completely. It is as if attending a masquerade party but wearing veils instead of masks.

I notice hundreds of candles have been set out. There are many different colors. All the colors of the rainbow and some in between, however, not only is the wax colored but so are the flames. The air is warm, wet and smoky. Some witches are talking in a low tone but all talking ceases and the room becomes quiet upon Emelie's arrival.

The witches promptly gather into formation and ready themselves for the impending ceremony. The circle embraces us forming a ring of witches. The witches hold hands. I grab Harley's hand. It feels tense and cold. Smoke builds up in the room, causing the candle light to refract and cast rainbow colors within the room. I look up to see the stained-glass of The Tree of Life. There is a soft light coming down from outside into the room.

Emelie speaks, "Witches of the light. We have gathered this hour to honor and accept these new students into our coven. Although they did not know, we have been watching them for decades. The time is right to offer them an apprenticeship with our coven. We welcome you, Harley, Lexa, Juni and Andi. You have many things in common with one another, including your interest in my introduction class at Safehaven College. However, our interest in you started long before college."

Emilie continues, "Do you girls remember getting a scholarship to Safehaven College?" We look at each other in a puzzled manner. "All of you girls were at the same honors convention during your junior year of high school. We scouted you out and approached each one of you in private to offer you a scholarship." I flash back to seventeen years old and remember that I was taken aside by a young woman and given a Certificate of Scholarship along with a necklace as a gift. The necklace was a tree, the sun and the moon inside a circle made out of silver. On the back of the necklace were the words "Safehaven College." I still have the necklace. I look at Harley, Juni and Lexa to see their reaction to this information. They look as shocked as I feel. To believe that we all attended the same convention, at the same time, without knowing it, was recruited by the same college, and then became best friends at Safehaven. This along with all the other new information I had been exposed to this weekend seemed to be too much. My mind races.

Emelie continues with the ceremony. "The candles are lit. We address the four corners: North South, East and West. We acknowledge Earth, Air, Fire and Water." Emelie places her finger in a chalice of salt water and sprinkles the water into the circle. "With this I purify the circle. The circle is closed." The robed witches step in closer to one another, physically closing the circle. I notice a large bowl inside the circle that contains various herbs, sand, salt, flowers and sliced pears.

Emelie asks, "Please repeat after me. I stand before the High

Priestess and accept her wisdom." All four of us repeat these powerful words. "I stand before our new sisters and brothers and accept them as family. I stand before the Goddess and Her eternal power. I stand before God and give service to His work. I pledge to respect the elements of Nature. I am a student of the Goddess and seek to perfect Her craft. My power comes from the Light and only the Light. My actions are for the Good and only the Good. My Magic comes from The Powers that Be. I devote myself to become a student of magic and a member of this coven. I pledge my loyalty to this coven. I pledge my efforts to improving this world. I will work endlessly to balance to the forces between Good and Evil: Light and Dark. As above, so below, like The Tree of Life. Power resides within us and outside of us. We give thanks and gratitude to our ancestors and continue their work on this earth. With this affirmation, I pledge an oath to serve with selflessness." We repeat her words in unison. "Now, I welcome you into our family. And so, it is." The coven hails, "And so, it is."

Emily pours clear wine into a chalice and rips a small piece of sweet bread off a loaf. She salutes the heavens above and then the earth below with her chalice. She addressed the four corners then takes a sip and places the piece of bread into her mouth. She savors the combination of the sweet bread and wine then passes the chalice and loaf of bread to each of us. The moon is high and it illuminates the purple stained glass. The purple light falls down upon the circle of witches.

Each of us gets a tattoo at the base of our neck. It is the roots of a tree. This symbolizes the first step of our apprenticeship and our initiation into the coven. We will subsequently get another part of the tree as we progress through the stages of training. Later, will come the trunk, the branches, the leaves and the fruit that make up The Tree of Life. Once we become 4rd degree witches, we will gain the ability to command "The Powers that Be." A night-long celebration follows our initiation. There is more food, wine, music, dancing and fellowship. It is a night I will never forget.

Chapter 6

Sid

Wasgard University is known for its' outdoor sculptures on campus. There are twenty-nine sculptures across the campus. Some are more obvious than others. Some are large and intrusive while other are small and diminutive. Some are titled, others untitled. This allows the viewer to assign her or his own meaning or value.

Professor Sid Swhart is particularly fond of a couple of sculptures on campus. One sculpture, simply called steam sculpture, as it is an unnamed piece of art. It discharges steam through a large bed of rocks. This sculpture is more apparent in the morning. The steam hits the cool morning air, creating large, white plumes of steam and mist. Another one of Sid's most favorites, is often compared to the ancient ruins of Stonehenge. It is called Stone Enclosure Rock Ring. Simply stated, it is a stone circle within a stone circle. The stones making up the walls are precisely cut and positioned. Within the circles of walls, circles are cut out making it possible to see through the sculpture from one side to the other. There are also archways cut out, like the circles, which are aligned perfectly through the four walls of the inner and outer circles. The campus folklore claims you can see the alignment of the sun through these circles at certain times of the year. This sculpture is a common meeting place for the Darksiders.

Dark witches thrive at night. Their powers are stronger at night, in contrast to the white witches whose powers are stronger in the day time when there is light. The dark witches are the sprinters of the witch world. They tend to be less disciplined and go for short but powerful bursts of magic. They spend less time studying their craft and more time experiencing and enjoying their magic in the physical world. Sid Swhart fits perfectly into this stereotype.

Sid is one of the older witches in his pack and the original witch that broke off from the white witch coven approximately thirty years ago. He was instrumental in starting the Darksiders. He saw no reason to study or practice the craft of white magic. He found that he could enhance his magical powers by using the dark forces. With this philosophy, he could gain access to the riches of the physical world.

Sid is the son of two white witches. Gertrude and Harry Madsen. He has a brother and a sister that he doesn't keep in touch with. He likes it better this way. More time and energy to focus on himself, without the distraction of family. Sid never married but fathered two children. He had another sister who is now deceased. He "earned" a Ph.D. but did so in a less honorable way than average. For Sid "possession is nine-tenths of the law." This is his operating philosophy and his degree is no exception to this rule.

Sid did not like to put off gratification. He wanted instant results and rewards. This is why he likes to play the stock market. He can buy stocks in the morning and see his profits grow by the end of the day. He dislikes waiting for long-term projects to pay off. It is easy money as far as he's concerned. It does not matter what stock he buys. The bottom line is money, not whether the stock is ethical or good for the world. What matters is profit. As can be predicted, Sid spends his money as soon as he "earns" it. Fast cars, fast women, fine restaurants, fine cigars, aged alcohol and other, not so moral or legal forms of consumption. This lifestyle seems to enrich his powers on a short-term basis, and therefore, this routine has become a circular pattern.

It is almost midnight as he walks across the campus. His Italian shoes make a clicking sound as they hit the bricks. The warmth of the night air arouses him. He can feel his energy rise, as it always does close to, and just after midnight. He is met by Nefara from one direction and Odious from another direction as three brick pathways intersect, making a triune of black. They quickly and concisely march across campus together toward the Rock Ring sculpture. Odious briefs Sid on his findings related to his surveillance of Emelie Walraven.

Sid expects his subordinates to report to him. They are his eyes, ears and muscle, as he is often distracted these days. There are far too many shinny objects, that are simply too enticing, to keep his attention on his pack. He loves the power connected to his position, including the compliance of his subordinates. Having others obey him without question gives him a rush. Then there is also the rush of using dark magic.

Odious briefs Sid that Emelie knows they discovered the code to the Ancient Library door. It is so simplistic, he thinks to himself. It's just like Emelie to use the date of the end of the Mayan calendar as a door code that protects the most sacred information and artifacts of her coven. Sid was only a second-degree white witch when he defected. Since he did not earn a more advanced degree, he never acquired full knowledge of "The Powers that Be." He couldn't help think that if he knew the rest of this information, he could use the most powerful white magic and most powerful dark magic together. This would make him the most powerful witch on either side. He knows that Lady Madsen's ashes are sacred to the white witches. Her ashes hold her DNA and her DNA hold the answers he seeks. Sid has some friends in the Biology Department who owe him favors and he intends to collect. Sid likes to redeem his favors, as he spends his money, as soon as he gets them.

The moon is bright and the three Darksiders cast a silhouette onto the field where the sculpture stands. As they approach the sculpture, others from their pack join them and situate themselves at various places inside the sculpture. Some are in the inner circle of the sculpture and others in the circles of the walls. They face Sid, Odious and Nefara and listen closely, as they are briefed. They repeat after Sid, as he releases a Delayed Dark Spell that rips through the night. In the distance is the ringing of a clock tower, as its' hands strike midnight. Like the white witches, the Darksiders also celebrate into the night but instead they make a point to defile the sculpture and disrespect all of the values associated with white magic.

Chapter 7

Hypatia Beach

I jolt awake at 7:00 am. It is my usual time to get up on a workday. I curse my internal clock. The dorm room is bright from the sun shining through the window. It's Sunday. My eyes are sore and swollen after the long night. My head is pounding due to too much wine and not enough sleep. I wish I could roll over and go back to sleep but I realize I am too awake for that. I notice a change in my perspective. My experience of the world seems changed and my viewpoint different. I feel enlightened, even in my compromised state. This feeling quickly disappears as a sudden uneasy sensation washes over me. I quickly recognize I have to run to the bathroom. I almost lose my bowels before reaching the toilet. Whatever I ate or drank last night did not agree with me. Lawren hears me moaning and asks if I am alright. "I'm okay." I grit my teeth as I say this, trying to ignore the pain and cramping in my gut. "It comes and goes in waves" I say from inside the stall.

I ask Lawren through clenched teeth "Did you enjoy the concert last night?" Lawren responds. "Yes, very much. I knew it was a surprise concert by an unannounced band but I didn't think the singer would stay anonymous. The lead singer wore an elaborate gown and veil that covered her face through the entire concert. So, in the end, I don't know who the surprise artist was. Another funny thing was that the warm up band played for hours and she didn't come on stage until after midnight. Anyway, I'm sorry you missed such a good concert." "Yeah, I know" I say. "You know Lawren, we should do something else together. I'm really sorry I couldn't go to the concert with you. It's just that my life has become more

Lawrence Anderson

complicated lately." Lawren appears to soften with these words. "Yes, Andi. I would really like that." "Hey" I say. "Guess what? I know of a perfect activity. Today is Basket Weaving with Natural Fibers and Drumming Circle. Wanna meet me there?" Lawren smiles, "I'll beat you to breakfast." I groan with pain as I pass gas with a new wave of cramps. I hope Lawren did not hear me.

Harley is still sleeping when I return to the dorm room. Suddenly Harley jolts out of bed and runs to the shared bathroom. I hear her yell "Shit!" After approximately 10 minutes, she returns and drops down on her bed. I tell her about what Lawren said about the surprise band. I ask Harley if she thinks it is a coincidence that the lead singer wore a "gown" and veil or were robes and veils suddenly in fashion?

Lawren obviously beats me to breakfast. Breakfast is the usual. Pale eggs, white, frozen then fried potatoes, frozen concentrate orange juice and pancakes with imitation maple syrup. "Now this is more like the food I remember" I say sarcastically. I can barely swallow it after yesterday's meals. I find that if I don't chew as much, it is easier to swallow. Then I remember it may also have something to do with how I was feeling earlier this morning.

Juni and Lexa arrive. They are late, making it just before the cafeteria stops serving. Lawren excuses herself to get more coffee.

The expression on Lexa's face is familiar. I joke, "Late night ladies?" Lexa looks at me as if to say "piss off" without saying a word. Juni says, "Lexa made friends with the Porcelain Goddess this morning." Juni continues, "Yeah, I literally had to pull her off the toilet, so I could use it." Lexa follows up with "That was the shits." She has no expression on her face when she says this, blunted by her sickness. "Juni must have ate different food. She is just fine." Juni says "Yes, I must have got lucky. I am just tired from the late night." I let them know that Harley and I also had nausea and diarrhea. "That was some party. Wasn't it?" Lexa adds, "I am going to think twice next time I'm invited to a witch party." I put my finger to my lips. Reminding Lexa to speak cautiously in her weakened state, with Lawren around. Lawren returns from getting coffee and sits down. She looks around the table. "Girls, you look awful. You must have had a good time last night. Although, last night Juni did say she was tired and Harley said she had a cough and wasn't feeling well. It must be contagious, as you all seem to have got the same thing." Lawren stuffs a forkful of greasy potatoes in her mouth, making Lexa cringe, as she watches. Lawren continues, "I hope I don't get it." Lexa says, "I'm pretty sure you won't, but I am not eating for a year." I smile at her and say "Nothing basket weaving can't cure." I grab her hand and pull her up into the direction of the workshop. Harley grabs several peppermint teas to go. "So, that we can sip and weave to calm our system." Lawren jumps up with the energy and enthusiasm of an evangelist and runs to the door. Juni follows her, the other three of us move much slower as we tag behind them.

The steps from the cafeteria to Safehaven College feel longer and steeper than usual. Lawren climbs to the top of the steps first. She turns around and looks down at us. She claps, cheering us on while trying to speed us up at the same time. She jumps up and down as each of us reaches the top of the stairs. Lexa flips her off when her back is turned.

We grab the chairs closest to the door and the bathroom. Just in case Mother Nature gives us a call without much notice. Lexa orders Lawren to the fifth chair furthest from the door, appearing a little irritated that Lawren does not feel sick like she does. Juni sits in the fourth chair, next to Lawren and snickers at Lexa.

I look up to see Emelie walk into the room. This is not an event that Emelie would normally attend. She smiles and grabs a chair then scoots next to me. We make room for her in the line of chairs. She greets everyone, as usual, including Lawren.

We grab different straws, grasses and yarns from the center of the circle. Some of the materials are dyed bright colors while others are left in their natural form. Emelie carefully starts her "spoke" for the bottom of her basket. She seems quite skillful to our surprise. She notices the green glow to our complexion and asks how we are doing with a concerned expression on her face. She smiles then leans in. "Girls, I forgot to tell you about the flu-like symptoms that you may get from the Initiation Ceremony. It is part of the cleansing process that happens when you move from one world to the next. In your case, you are moving from the mortal world to the world of the white witch. Your energy changes and this causes your body to purge long held toxins that are physical, spiritual and emotional." She jokes, "It could also be the effects of Edwards's fermented tea. But it was good, wasn't it?"

"Anyhow, since the dark forces have learned the combination to the Ancient Library, we have had to change the code. The Darksiders are trying to get the former High Priestess' crematory ashes. They have been trying to find the source of our magical power but have been unsuccessful. They think the High Priestess' ashes will help them find out. Luckily, we have long buried her ashes in a safe and sacred place."

Lawren notices that Emelie is talking quietly to the four of us, leaving her out of the conversation. I can tell she feels hurt and left out. Lawren slides her chair closer to us but Emelie speaks even softer. Lawren frowns. Emelie continues. "The Darksiders are becoming more flagrant in their escalation towards us. Meet me at Hypatia Beach this afternoon. I will tell you more at that time." Emelie smiles at Lawren and excuses herself. Lawren's upset seems to dissolve.

I look at the others, noting the progress of their baskets. Harley hasn't even started her spoke yet. She appears to have made several attempts without any significant progress. Harley picks up Emelie's spoke that she left behind. Harley smiles and continues to add to Emelie's spoke. Lexa grabs it from Harley and starts weaving on it. I start my spoke from purple yarn. For some reason, I feel particularly drawn to this color. I think to myself that this basket will be the centerpiece of my living room.

We take our treasured, though partially complete, baskets to the drumming circle. We vigorously play various instruments then stop and return to the weaving circle. We go back and forth between weaving and drumming. Lexa pretends to play her, or I should say Emelie's basket, as if it were a drum. It's Lexa's version of Air Guitar. Lawren excuses herself to go to the "womyn's bathroom." I signal to the others to follow me, taking advantage of Lawren's exit. Harley asks, "Is this why you kept encouraging Lawren to drink the coffee? I was puzzled when you kept saying it was so good. It makes sense now. We can talk during her bathroom breaks." We leave the circle with our coveted baskets and head toward the parking lot. We walk then run to Harley's Hybrid, looking back to make sure Lawren hasn't seen us.

All of us squeeze into the eco-car. Lexa and Juni sit in the backseat with their baskets sitting proudly on their laps. I gaze at my purple basket with pride. Harley pulls out of the parking stall and begins to drive away before she realizes she left her basket on top of the car. She stops and reaches out the window and grasps it carefully. She appears relieved it is safe. She floors the hybrid. Its thin wheels spin out, leaving thin burnout marks in the gravel. I let out a sigh of relief as we escape without detection.

We drive south, down Mystics Drive. The view of the bay is beautiful and relaxing. We pass Adelina Beach. Simultaneously we all turn to see if we can see any nude people on the beach from the main road. No such luck. The nudists must be lying down on their beach towels instead of standing. We continue approximately five miles then park the car. It is a hike to the beach unlike most of the beaches in the area. The trail is lined with heavy shrubbery. Once we get off the trail, we hit large dunes of light brown, almost white sand. It is a sunny day. I feel the sun's heat radiate off the sand and warm my body. I take off my shoes and continue to walk with my bare feet. My calves work extra hard in the loose sand. I follow the others, as I am not able to walk as fast without shoes. Juni asks "Where is she? It's after 1:00 pm." Harley sits down on the sand enjoying the day. She lets her head fall back and closes her eyes. "This feels good after such a long night." Lexa is standing next to her. She squirms, crosses her legs, grabs her crotch, then runs into the bushes, squatting. She barely gets her pants down in time.

I gaze out at the water. At first, I think I am looking at the remnants of an old pier but realize it is a tall, thin person standing knee deep in the saltwater. Her pants are rolled up to her knees, her hair and overshirt are blowing in the breeze. I nudge Harley and point at Emelie. The others look out. We immediately roll up our pants and walk out to the sandbar leading to where Emelie is standing. She appears internally preoccupied. I call out her name. She quietly announces she knew we were there before we noticed her.

Emelie talks with her eyes closed. "Our powers are heightened by contact with the bare earth, tall trees and water, but especially saltwater." I had noticed an odd sensation going through my body but thought it was the effects of the cool water on my warm skin. Emelie asks, "Do you feel it? Now, hold each other's hand." I feel another change in energy in my body. "Now, hold my hand." Again, I feel an increased sensation and intensity of energy flowing through my body. "I come out here to clear my head and feel close to nature." We stand in a circle, holding hands in the water. Emelie continues, "White witches tap into the natural forces of energy to supply and regenerate their powers. This is why our craft is so connected to nature. It is the source of our power. Our power is subtle. It works with other natural forces, in synergy. We are energetic beings, as are all living things. Yes, we have chemistry but we are also energy.

Our energetic forces are much quicker and more efficient than our chemistry. You know in physics when you learn that light is both a wave and a particle at the same time? Well, the body is both chemical and energetic, however, energy travels at the speed of light versus the slow pace of chemicals, like hormones in our body. White witches use both. We use chemicals, such as herbs but the primary outcome is to change the energy of something, so we can heal or vibrate on a healthier frequency. This is also done by using spells. And, ladies, a spell is only a form of prayer. Just like the ones used by other religions and spiritual practices. We too use the power of the Goddess or God with addition to the power of nature. Yes, there are dark powers and light powers. The world is balanced by opposing forces. You can see this pattern throughout nature such as in our bodies, in plants and animals, in space and the universe. The earth only mimics the laws of the universe. Our coven only uses the light forces. We never dabble in the dark forces. There are consequences for disturbing the natural order of the opposing forces. As you change or correct one force, the opposite force is affected. Nature is constantly seeking an equilibrium. Therefore, we have to be aware of the consequences of our actions.

"As far as stereotypes go, white witches do not have large, crooked noses. We don't typically use wands and I hope you are not

Lawrence Anderson

too disappointed, we don't ride brooms either", Emelie laughs. "There are origins of these myths. For example, some witches use brooms to clean or clear a sacred place, either physically or energetically, prior to a ceremony or worship. And a wand may have historically been used as a symbol of power, royalty or divinity but is also a means to focus power, like an antenna. In any event, we commonly use neither. As far as the pointed hats are concerned, these are associated with the Jewish tradition centuries ago, not witches. As you are all aware, various persons and leaders have been known to use stereotypes to change public attitudes and the status of others by revising history, truth and culture.

"Do you feel the energy in your palms? This is our energy port. Let me teach you your first spell. It is a protection spell. This will deflect negative energy or reduce its' impact. Turn your backs into the circle. We will now face outward. This protects our backs and the sacredness of our circle. Raise your palms up while still keeping contact with your neighbor's hand. Just like any other animal, our back is one of our vulnerable spots. We must protect our backs. Always face you aggressor. Now, repeat after me: The circle is cast around us. We are safe from the ill-doers who have found us. Use nature's synergy to protect us from injury. Shielding our presence from those who seek to offend us. Divert and send back their dark energy." The four of us repeat the spell. "Words of a spell are important but more so, is intent. Certain spells have been used for centuries and have cumulative powers. Just like our neural pathways get more entrenched as we use them. So, do spells. In addition to words of the spell, picture the outcome you want and see it happen in your mind's eye. Then announce 'I set this in motion for the good and only the good. And so, it is.'" We repeat after Emelie. She reminds us, "Now, I will see you at the Farewell Luncheon at Safehaven." Lexa repeats "Now, I will see you at the Farewell Luncheon at Safehaven." She slowly opens her eyes when she realizes she is the only one repeating this sentence. We stare at her with incredulity as she breaks the sanctity of our ritual.

We leave Emelie standing in the water with her eyes closed. A salty breeze lifts off the bay as we head back on the trail toward our car. It seems like just minutes on the trial before we reach the car, even though I know we hiked at least a mile.

We drive back to the dorms to freshen up. I shower quickly to get the sand out from between my toes and salt off my legs before the luncheon. I sit on my bed talking to Harley as I dry my hair with a towel. "Where is Lawren?" Harley asks. "I don't know", I say. I hear a noise outside in the hallway and get up to see if it's Lawren. I open the door and look out. Everything is quiet with no sign of activity. I'm puzzled by the thought of what could have made the noise. I turn to close the door. Out of the corner of my eye, I see a black streak. I look down to see a little kitten darting through the closing door and into our dorm room. It is a cute, black, long haired kitten with a short nose and a wide face. Her eyes are large and golden yellow. She jumps up onto my bed and lays down. She meows in a low tone that is cute and endearing. "Oh, little kitty" I say to her. "Where did you come from?" The cat kneads my bedding then gets up purring and rubs against me. I quickly grab her and hold her close. She purrs louder, raising her head so I can scratch under her chin. I put her down on the bed being concerned that I may squeeze her too tight. The little kitten starts batting at my hand with her little sharp claws. She arches her back, walks sideways with her fur standing straight up on her back. Her tail sticks straight up also and becomes full. It is clear she is playing with me as if I were another kitten or her mother. I wonder if she was abandoned or lost. She continues to purr loudly. I walk over to the refrigerator to see what I can feed her. There is nothing suitable for a cat. I grab my coat and go through the pockets. I find leftover cat treats from my two cats at home. Langston and Sebastian would be very upset if they knew I was feeding another cat. Langston is a beautiful gray Persian and has similar features as the black kitten. Persians are my favorite cats. They are loving and sweet. My other cat is a Tabby. He is black, brown and gray with dark stripes and white patches. He is the hunter of the family.

I say to Harley "It is so unusual that someone would let such a beautiful kitten out by itself. I can't let her roam around unprotected. She seems to be hungry." The cat gobbles down the treat and looks intently at me as if to say she wants another. Harley grabs her, kisses her face then puts her in my shirt. We leave to go to the luncheon.

We step onto the brick pathway that leads toward the outdoor patio at Safehaven. The day is warming up. I notice there is a slight breeze that carries the aroma of lunch. The menu consists of various Mexican entrées and the combined aromas are appetizing. I see that Emelie, Edward, Lexa and Juni already have plates of food and are sitting out on the patio. Edward has brought some more wine and fermented tea. I sample both. I think to myself that since I became a

"real witch" my tastes have changed. I get a full glass of fermented tea and sit down.

The little black kitten's claws stick me under my shirt. I make a face from the pain. Emelie looks concerned. I tell her the story of how the cat darted into our dorm room from the hallway. Lexa jokes about the black cat crossing my path and the years of bad luck I will receive. Emelie says "She is your familiar." I say, "My what?" "You're familiar. This is the animal helper that finds you. You did say this cat came out of nowhere." "Yes, she did." The others look at the cat and start talking baby talk and petting her. Lexa mentions, "I hear that cats are not afraid to die." Emelie adds, "Isn't it ironic that they have nine lives?" I sneak the little cat some food from my plate. "At least we know she has a healthy appetite." "And loves Mexican food as much as we do", Juni finishes my sentence.

Lawren shows up and joins us at the table. She grabs the chair next to me. She turns as she puts her jacket over her chair. I, Harley, Lexa and Juni laugh loudly. Lawren whips around, "What? What?" Lexa points to a sock that has secured itself to the Velcro of her hiking shorts. Lawren's face turns red. She lists all the places she has been today with the sock on the back of her shorts and nobody told her. "I wondered why everyone was snickering around me today." She continues, "At least it is clean. I did my laundry in the dorms." She tugs hard on the sock. It makes a loud ripping noise as it disengages from the Velcro. She quickly puts the sock in her jacket pocket to avoid further embarrassment.

Juni gets up and walks toward the stage that has been constructed on the patio. We watch her thinking she may have drunk too much, though we did not see her drinking alcohol. She grabs a mic and introduces herself as a graduate of Safehaven some thirty years ago. She talks about her major in Business and her minor in Music. She sits down at the piano and starts playing. Her voice is beautiful. She is able to sing the low, soft and silky blues notes and the high, glass shattering notes. She chants a silly song about Safehaven using several octaves. Her piano playing is influenced by her classical training. In her song, she includes the names of all the professors who influenced her education and humorously cites various stereotypes of Safehaven. The audience laughs and applauds in gratitude.

"I didn't know Juni was so talented", I say. Juni returns to the group. We all compliment her. Juni responds, "Really, it was nothing.

I have sung in public many times." Harley comments "You should get an agent." She smiles coyly.

Emelie goes to the stage to give updates on Safehaven. She talks about the professors on sabbaticals, those who have authored publications, received awards, those who are retiring and those who have already retired. As she is talking, I look up to see Harley coming at me with a doughnut in her hand. She takes the doughnut and smashes it in my face. I am surprised at her behavior, as she is clearly possessing ill-intent. Harley announces, "All cops like donuts." Suddenly, I spout out, "You're just sore from hugging too many trees." I am confused as to why these words came out of my mouth. Then I look at Lexa, who is holding the black kitten. I announce "That is the only pussy you're going to get." Lexa looks at Juni and says, "You put the black into black magic." Juni returns back to Lexa, "I would have made a better basketball player." Lexa retorts, "Look who's is singing the blues now." Juni says to Lexa, "Look who's been benched." Emelie is still giving her presentation and is trying to talk over all the chaos. Juni throws an enchilada at Lexa and Lexa throws some sour cream back hitting Juni in the face. Harley hurls some refried beans at me. I throw a glass of fermented tea at her. Emelie quickly finishes and introduces the next speaker. She steps off the stage and heads toward our table. We are shocked by our behavior but can't seem to stop it. Emelie whispers to us. "It's a spell. Engage your protection spell." She pushes us in a circle and forces us to hold hands. We recite the spell quietly, "The circle is cast around us. We are safe from the ill-doers who have found us. Use nature's synergy to protect us from injury. Shielding our presence from those who seek to offend us. Divert and send back their dark energy. I set this in motion for the good and only the good. And so, it is." Instantly, we come our senses. I feel my face turn red in embarrassment as I realize how disruptive we were. Our table is littered with food and our clothes are soiled. Emelie escorts us to our dorms.

Chapter 8

Ashes to Ashes

After a shower I meet the others in the Truth Hall lounge. I have a towel around my shoulders from showering. Harley is in her bathrobe. Lexa is wearing Wasgard sweats and Juni is wearing big fuzzy slippers. We apologize to each other and talk about the feelings we experienced while we were under the spell. Lexa states just before the spell, she felt like she was going to get Montezuma's Revenge. We all acknowledge how destructive the spell could have been to our friendship. We vow not to let dark magic affect our relationships. We all concur that we need more witch training. I promise to contact Emelie with our request.

As I was return to my dorm, I realize, I don't know how to contact Emelie. Since I couldn't let the others down, I head toward the Biodynamic Farm. I figure Edward can tell me how to get ahold of her.

Edward is at the Learning Center. He is mixing herbs and placing this mixture in small baggies. Each baggie is labeled. One baggie says "Healing", another, "Lost Memory", another "Time/Space", "60 Second Delay" and another baggie says "Protection." I ask Edward if the Protection herbs would strengthen our protection spell. Edward says that the herbs enhance magic. "They are an additional tool that helps the energy and natural forces find their way easier and accentuate one's power." He points to the herbs in the Protection baggie. "This is wolvestail, ginger, cedar and passion flower." He hands me baggies of the various mixtures. "You may need these after the incident earlier today. You will become better at recognizing black magic when you see it. You should always be prepared." He

winks then smiles. I open a baggie to smell it. It's aromatic and sweet smelling. I close my eyes and breathe it in, then close up the baggie and stick it into my shirt pocket with the others baggies.

As I look up, Emelie appears, again, out of nowhere. I tell her I was looking for her. She smiled and says, "I know." She tells me that she has already informed the others of a "special gathering." I can see Harley, Lexa and Juni walking toward the pharm from the dorms. Emelie is silent until they join us.

Emelie looks at Edward as she talks. "I broke the Witches Code of Conduct. I didn't tell the truth about burying the ashes of the former High Priestess. It is with great sadness that I have to inform you that the High Priestess' ashes have been stolen! We must get the ashes back before the Darksiders can find a way to read the ashes and gain inside knowledge into our coven. Specifically, the mystery of our powers. I need your help. There are rumors that our coven has been infiltrated by the Darksiders. Therefore, I cannot trust anyone, except you girls and Edward until we sort all this out. The tension between the dark and white witches are at their height. Our conflict goes back several decades. It is suspected that the dark forces have secured one of the professors in the Biology Department. There are a couple on staff that we suspect." Edward nods as Emelie speaks. "Dr. Luciana Santiago is a geneticist and Dr. Eric Slater is a microbiologist. Both are doing research in the same field. They are the only ones who would have the knowledge to assist Dr. Swhart. You four are going to receive the quickest witches training that ever existed."

Edward pours some fresh tea from a steaming teapot sitting over the fire. The tea is hot and flavorful. I assume the herbs are freshly picked. Edward proudly reports the tea is a combination of green tea, mint and American Ginseng from the pharm.

Emelie gets our attention. "I must give you a condensed training before the Fund-Raising Dinner tonight. Representatives from the Biology Department will be present at this event. To cast a spell, you must use the free energy in the universe. You have to redirect and guide the energy that already exists. You direct this energy to do what you want it to do. Nikola Tesla was an inventor in the late 1800's. He found in order to receive free energy from the universe, one must tune to the energy one wants to receive. This is why dark witches do evil deeds. They are tuned to the dark energy. And we, as white witches, stay tuned to the frequency of good energy and therefore, do good deeds. You will become better at harnessing this energy with practice. Say a prayer and ask the Goddess or Nature for help. They are one in the same. Animals are also helpful. What is your black cat's name?" I answer, "Samantha", as this name just pops into my head. "I will call her Sam for short", I say automatically as if someone is whispering this information in my ear. Sam starts purring loudly. Emelie says, "I hope you all find your animal helpers. They should present themselves to you. Now, follow me. Remember your palms are your energy ports. Also, remember to say the words of the spell then imagine your desired outcome in your mind's eye. The outcome is always For the Good and Only the Good. Ask the Goddess, Nature, your animal helpers and the free energy of the universe for help. Then say And So It Is. Let the energy field do the rest. When using this energy, time is not linear. Therefore, you can reverse any situation by using a time/space spell. By disconnecting the connection between time and space you can go back in time and change an outcome. Don't forget what you put out into the universe comes back threefold. So be careful. Now we must sit quietly and meditate. We have a lot of hard work to do tonight."

Emelie guides us in meditation. As I sit quietly in the circle, Emelie comes from behind, touches me lightly on the shoulder and whispers into my ear. "What is your craft name?" Instantly, a name pops into my head. She goes on to each of the others and asks the same question. Emelie guides us in imagining a good outcome tonight then gently pulls us out of our meditative state.

I slowly open my eyes and come back to the external world. My thought process is focused, confident and peaceful. Lexa sits across from me in the circle. I see her jump forward and then let out a scream. Behind her is a potbelly pig nudging her with its snout. She turns around to examine the swine. She whimpers, "No! No! It can't be! My familiar is a pig? I guess we can pig-out together, roll in the mud, make bacon, wear the same lipstick. Yeah, when pigs fly." Emelie interrupts Lexa's tirade to say "You don't pick your animal helper. They pick you." Edward rubs the head of the friendly goat beside him and Emelie looks outward to the trees where her red fox sits observing us from afar.

It's mid-afternoon and things are winding down on campus. Many of the alumni are heading home. We head back to our dorm. Lawren is sitting in the lounge. She wonders where we were without her. I explain that we had to pick some fresh herbs at the pharm to treat the symptoms we had earlier. I assure her, "We are all feeling much better." The other three nod zealously confirming they are feeling better. Lawren says, "Great. I kind of have a headache. Can I have some of those herbs?" I stutter, "Uh, um…Yeah" I am set aback by her request, then remember. I reach into my shirt pocket and pull out a packet of herbs that Edward gave me. I hand it to her. She thanks me and heads toward her dorm room to get hot water to brew the tea. I ask her if she is going to the Fund-Raising Dinner later, though I call it the "Donation Dinner." Lawren says she is planning on going as she heads toward dorm room #10.

We quickly leave as she exits the lounge. She returns with a steaming cup of steeping tea. She is talking, looks up and stops in her place. She realizes we had left. She stops talking mid-sentence as there is no one to hear her.

The four of us circle back and meet in Harley's and my dorm. I ask Juni, "What is your Craft Name?" Juni replies, "I had a sensation of smelling the herb Sage." Harley says "I saw an image of a new moon and the word Neona came into my head." I told the group my name was Orenda and this name was associated with a feeling of universal power and being connected to all living things "So, Lexa", I inquire, "What is your craft name?" Lexa looks upset. She says something under her breath. It was so soft we couldn't hear her. I ask, "Can you speak a little louder?" Lexa raises her voice, "Medusa." We all look at each other and laugh loudly. Lexa fakes a cough, saying "Witches with a capital B" in a slightly camouflaged manner, referring to us. "We will have to work on your craft name but for now we will call you Ducia which is short for Medusa."

"Well, let's prepare for battle." The others look at me in a perplexed manner. Juni says, "We have never been to battle before. How do we prepare?" I reflect and decide that this is a good question. I think of the history I learned in high school. Of course, this type of history is always about men and war. I reply, "Check your weapons and equipment." Juni responds, "We don't have any weapons or equipment." Juni stands looking at me in a sarcastic manner. I think and add carefully "Dress yourself in your uniform?" I realize this is even less helpful, as such dress would draw attention to us. Then I add, "Say a prayer. Say good-bye to your family and friends." Juni thanks me for my most thoughtful and helpful advice. "Seriously", I say, "Let's sit, hold hands and meditate on it." I turn down the lights and open a window to let in fresh air. I guide the group through a meditation similar to the one Emelie used earlier today. I asked for help from the Goddess, the natural forces in the universe and for the former High Priestess to guide us on our mission. I want to add Lexa's Potbelly pig but I knew this was a serious mission and humor would be inappropriate at this time.

I allow my mind to open to any response I may get from these sources. I wait in silence. Then an image comes into my head. In my mind's eye, I am quickly moving through a dark tunnel until I reach a dark room. The word "white" comes into my head. I see the woman who said this word to me. She identifies herself as "Gertrude." Suddenly I come back. My eyes open wide. I look around at the others. They quickly open their eyes as well. Our hands release their grasp, breaking the circle.

The Donation Dinner is a fundraising event that is heavy on the fundraising and light on dinner. The event is early at 4:30 pm. It is the last formal event of the reunion weekend. Soon all the visitors will be gone and the campus quiet, like a ghost town, until late September when the students return. The dinner is held at the Commons cafeteria which is at the northern end of campus. The cafeteria had a complete makeover from the typical decor for the students during the school year. The tables are decorated with formal white tablecloths, napkins and plates. There is fine cutlery, wine glasses, candles and eye-catching garnish on the tables. Name tags on the tables identify different colleges on the university. The attendees are dressed in formal clothing with flashy jewelry. I knew there was a reason I usually skipped this event, besides not wanting to sit through the long sales pitch by The Endowment. I don't mind giving to the university. It was my way of giving back for all I have received from my education at Safehaven College. I am so grateful for the experiences I had on this campus and I really want to see the unique curriculum at Safehaven continue. I just feel the money-drive really changes the focus from a community reunion to a fund-raising event. But back to my current task at hand. I look around the cafeteria to get my bearings.

We shuffle toward the table labeled "Safehaven College." Clearly those already sitting at this table are under-dressed in comparison to the other tables. Across the cafeteria, I see the table for the Biology Department. The biology professors are all sitting together. I wonder which one is Dr. Santiago and Dr. Slater out of the numerous professors sitting around the table. A student working as a server places a dinner plate in front of me with a rare cooked steak on it.

I politely ask for the vegetarian meal. She looks at me as if to say
I fit the stereotype of a Safehaven Alumni. I grab a cup of coffee
from another server. It seems that most of those sitting at the other
tables are drinking white wine instead of coffee. I ask the server for a
nondairy creamer. She says, "Yes, but I cannot guarantee is it organic,
gluten free or vegan" in a sarcastic tone. I let out a contemptuous
chuckle. Later I will spill my coffee all over the white drapery and rug
in a passive-aggressive act. Harley scratches her nose with her middle
finger as she stares down the server. Lexa puts her arm around Juni
and acts as if they are lovers in an outward show of lesbian affection
in Safehaven fashion. I tell myself to refocus on the task at hand.

Each Department takes their turn presenting the status of their
department, their research and possible implications for grants
and endowments within their department. The head of the Biology
Department stands up and introduces Dr. Santiago and Dr. Slater.

The two describe their research reading secondary information
from DNA strands. This reading is derived by measuring the charge
and emission of each nucleotide in the DNA configuration.

Dr. Slater stands tall, even though he is only about five foot seven
inches tall. He puffs out his chest as he speaks. His voice is higher
in tone than expected. His thinning brown hair is meticulously cut
and appears to have been dyed. He describes his research much like
the binary numbers used in computer programing and computer
memory.

Dr. Santiago smiles as Dr. Slater speaks. She has a pretty smile
that she tries to guise. She pulls back her curly black hair, gathers it
and lets it drop down her back. She begins where Dr. Slater leaves
off. She reports she feels this type of decoding will be available to
the community within the next decade. She states, "We will soon
be able to read not only the fixed genetic code, but the epigenetic
information that influences and changes the expression of the DNA
as it responds to the environment. We could read DNA to understand
how learning, lifestyle choices and culture effects our genes. This
tool may become common place in our society." She appears uneasy
in front of such a large gathering. The audience claps loudly for
an extended period of time, conveying their enthusiasm for this
research.

"At least we now have faces to the names." I say to the others. Dr.
Slater announces that the Biology Department will be having a tour
of their research laboratory after the dinner. He encourages everyone

to donate money to support further research in this field. My eyes are drawn to a particularly enthusiastic table next to the Biology Department. The name plate identifies the table as the Business College. I can see Dr. Swhart and his graduate students, sitting at the table along with the other business professors.

I attempt to eat my over-priced, Donation Dinner. It is the vegetarian option but is very dry. It seems to have sat in the refrigerator for an extended period of time waiting for a vegetarian to claim it. I take a gulp of my coffee to rehydrate the contents in my mouth but the coffee is bitter. I forcibly swallow, so I don't involuntarily spit it out onto the table in front of others. It takes a couple of swallows to do this.

Emelie shows up late to give her speech on Safehaven College. She speaks on how Safehaven's approach to education is different from conventional learning and how Safehaven values the process of learning rather than just the student's grades. She talks about specific students who have become accomplished after graduation. As she elaborates, the audience seems distracted and loud, talking amongst themselves. Dr. Swhart interrupts Emelie to ask for statistics on the average wages of Safehaven graduates. Emelie admits that Safehaven graduates tend to make a little less money than the average graduate. However, she points out that there are qualitative factors, as well as quantitative factors to consider, such as job satisfaction and the benefit to society. She comments that she is considering developing a system which ranks different factors similar to the system Dr. Swhart uses in business but focusing on factors associated with quality of life versus economics. She then thanks Dr. Swhart for his question but refers to him as Sid instead of Dr. Swhart. Sid turns a deep shade of red but does not challenge Emelie further. Emelie ends her talk with a Question and Answer period. I notice the look Odious gives Emelie. Odious is sitting next to Sid. "If looks could kill" I say to Harley. I look across the room to see Edward standing at the doorway.

Emelie and Edward join our table after her presentation. She informs us that she and Edward will distract Dr. Slater and Dr. Santiago during the tour while we search for the former High Priestess' ashes. At this point, I look up to see Odious, Nefara and Alan, the Business Departments graduate students, approach our table. Emelie keeps them in her line of sight. Odious asks me if I want to get a drink after dinner. At the same time, Alan approaches Lexa and stands too close to her, invading her personal space. He wears his delicate light brown hair in a spike with the support of a generous amount of hair wax.

I apologetically decline Odious 'offer, informing him that we have an engagement after dinner. My tone is abrupt as I move toward the door. The others follow. Odious adds, "The offer is always open."

I whisper to the others, "He really creeps me out and to think I was alone in the Ancient Library with him." I make a faint gagging sound. Lexa says, "Yeah, right, I would go out with that Alan dude! He doesn't even know he is barking up the wrong tree, on the wrong side of the fence and playing for the wrong team, using mustard versus ketchup…"

We follow Dr. Slater and Dr. Santiago along with the other alumni from the Donation Dinner as we walk toward the Biology Department. After a short distance, we hear a loud cracking noise. I look side to side then upward, trying to locate the origin of the sound. I look up again at the blue sky and catch a bolt of lightning move across the sky and branch out in all directions. I see the others are also startled. I ready myself but there is no more thunder to follow. I see Odious, Nefara and Alan in the back of the group. "I thought they were going for drinks?" Harley comments "It looks like they had enough to drink at dinner." I see an unsteadiness to their gait. Juni leans in, "Leave this to me." Juni heads to the back of the group where the entourage is amassed. Emelie and Edward engage the Biology professors. We continue walking toward the southern part of campus and turn into a cement building with the letters SMT above the threshold, identifying it as the Science, Math and Technology College. We follow the group down the cement stairs to room B-66, in the basement. Harley exclaims, "This is what came into my mind during our meditation, B66. I didn't know what it meant until now."

There are all types of sophisticated analytical instruments in the lab. This would explain the lack of windows. Dr. Slater boasts about his Capillary Analyzer, his Infrared Spectrometer and his new Ultra Performance Liquid Chromatograph. Dr. Santiago is talking to other alumni but pauses to interject, "This is where we do our magic." She smiles at the group as she speaks. Edward starts asking questions about analyzing plant extracts and how other researchers are working on discovering medicinal compounds in certain plants. This is his way of distracting the two. Both Dr. Slater and Dr. Santiago get involved in the conversation. Dr. Slater talks about specific types of antioxidants in plants. Dr. Santiago adds she has gone to different countries and studied medicinal plants under various Shaman. She announces this type of research is close to her heart.

Juni is talking to the three business grads. She seems to be flirting with all three, including Nefara, who appears to be enjoying it. They don't seem to care about her age, gender or other differences. Who could blame them? Juni is beautiful.

This was our cue to try and find where the samples are stored. Harley said Dr. Santiago pointed across the room when she was talking about her process of getting a sample and preparing it for analysis. "You know when Dr. Slater was talking and boring everyone with the description of his expensive instruments." The three of us head toward a side room where there are microscopes, automatic pipettes and several large refrigerators. "Look for anything that looks like ashes. You two take that refrigerator. I will take this one. If you are unsure, take the sample anyway."

I open the door of a large refrigerator. It was categorized. All drawers are labeled. I run my finger across all the small drawers as I read the labels. No label with the words "Former High Priestess' Ashes." This was no surprise. There are a few unlabeled drawers but nothing is in them. I continue to look then find a secured drawer with a combination lock. Just then, Harley and Lexa join me. I show them the combination lock. "How are we supposed to open this?" Lexa recites, "15327." "What?" I say. Lexa talks in a high-pitched voice, "This is what came to me during our meditation." I hurry and enter 15-32-7. The secure drawer opens. We celebrate quietly. I pull out a large sample that is powdery with large mineral compounds in it. I grab the sample. I say, "Let's get out of here." As we turn to leave, I look up to see a woman standing in the doorway. By the looks of her uniform and her arm patch, I surmise she is campus police. Her name tag says, "S. Tandori." She is obviously of Southern Asian descent. Her hair is wavy, thick and black. Her eyes are dark brown and her skin is the color of reddish-brown clay. She stands in an open stance. Her build is athletic. She addresses us. "Ladies, are you enjoying your tour? You know we have had several reports of theft lately. You ladies wouldn't happen to know anything about this, would you?" "No ma'am." Lexa pulls out a peanut butter and jelly sandwich from her pocket and takes a big bite. "I am a grad student helping with research. I left my lunch here and was hungry. So, I came back to get it. I am so glad it was still here. Mmmm, it is so good. Want a bite? You can't trust other grad students not to steal your lunch. Thank you so much for protecting my lunch." "Let me escort you back to the group", Officer Tandori offers. We walk back to the tour group.

I poke Lexa with my elbow as we walk. "What were you doing in there?" Lexa replies, "My stomach was upset. So, I took someone's lunch hoping it would make me feel better. You said, if we were unsure, take it anyway. I was unsure whether I would feel alright without something in my stomach."

Edward is asking whether chlorophyll interferes with the instruments' chemical analysis. Emelie whispers, "I am glad you are back. Edward is running out of questions." Emelie says aloud, "Ah, I see you met Officer Tandori. Shamita, this is Andi, Harley, Lexa and Juni is over there." Lexa is still eating her stolen sandwich. "Nice to formally meet you ladies. Emelie, will you take it from here?" "Yes", Emelie replies, "And I will make sure they bring lunch money next time." Officer Tandori, winks and walks away.

Once Juni sees we had re-grouped, she breaks off her conversation with the grad students. They appear disappointed. Juni is known to be a smooth talker. Juni doesn't feel bad for them. "I am sure they are here to represent the Darksiders, and distract us. We just turned it around on them. I also gained some intelligence. They are meeting tonight at the steam sculpture on campus. This slipped out of Nefara's mouth. She cannot hold her liquor." I ask, "Juni, did you get any messages during our meditation?" She shakes her head, "Yeah but I don't understand. The letters ATCG came into my head." Harley pipes up, "Of course, Adenine, Thymine, Cytosine and Guanine." We look at Harley in a puzzled manner. "These are the nucleic acids that make up DNA." Lexa exclaims, "I knew that. Yeah, knew that!" in an unconvincing manner. I bring up a fist, showing my knuckles for a knuckle bump. The others respond by doing the same. We exchange knuckle bumps. Emelie isn't quite sure how to do this but modeled the others in an inept way. She clears her throat, "A job well done."

Chapter 9

Premonition, Dreams and Meditation

We meet back at the Biodynamic Farm. Edward has started a fire and is brewing tea. We sit around the fire in a circle. We continue to celebrate the recovery of the former High Priestess' ashes. We toast loudly over the fire. Emelie changes her volume to a low tone. "Today you learned and applied new techniques. You did really well but this is not over. Once the Darksiders realize we stole back the former High Priestess' ashes, they will retaliate. Keep on your toes and continue your training. Tonight, we will work with changing energy. Emelie sits numerous candles by the fire. She speaks a name every time she lights a candle then opens her palms toward the flames of the fire. The flames extinguish. She then opens and waves her hands again and the smoking logs burst into flames. Edward takes out some herbs and throws them into the fire. The flames turn blue, red, and purple then repeat these colors in succession. "Every night I address my ancestors, relatives and friends and those who have influenced my life including my animal helpers." In the distance, I can hear the soft sound of a barking fox. I give Sam a quick hug. She purrs inside my jacket. I ask Lexa where is her pig. Edward opens a gate and the potbelly pig and goat come out running together. The pig is playing with the goat as if they are two of the same.

Edward serves more tea. It steams as he pours it into our blue enamel cups. Emelie speaks, "We are drinking Jasmine tea in honor of those who have not found their animal helper. May your animal helper find you to offer their service. Jasmine encourages spiritual guides to come forward. This is to you, Juni and Harley." We toast. It always amazes me how tea tastes better around the campfire.

"Lexa, I know you're disappointed with your animal helper. However, in many ancient cultures, the pig symbolizes sincerity, honesty, abundance and fertility. Those are all good qualities. And as far as your craft name goes, Ducia means you are pleasant, friendly, personable and funny. Your animal helper and your craft name honor you." Lexa pauses to sincerely reply. "You know; Potbelly is really growing on me. Look at her little tail wagging like a dog's tail and watching her try to jump like a little goat is so endearing. Her little oinking and snorting is so cute. Oh, come here you." The pig stops playing with the goat and runs up to Lexa. "Who's my piggy? Should I give her a proper name? How about Ms. Piggy?" Lexa laughs looking at the pig. "You look like... a...Susy." She leans over to hug her. You are just a big Sus." The little pig grunts in delight. "Oh, don't get too close to the camp fire, or you may become dinner. No luau for you." Edward winks. "The pig family is Suidae and the genus is Sus. This is a great name for a happy pig."

Emelie speaks. "We still don't know whether it is Dr. Slater or Dr. Santiago who is working with the Darksiders." I speak up, "Emelie, maybe we should spy on the Darksiders tonight, at the steam sculpture. Maybe we can get intelligence on their plan for revenge or which professor is the working with them. The best defensive is a good offense."

"You know, as the High Priestess, I cannot accompany you." Edward finishes for Emelie. "We must keep Emelie safe and protected." Emelie waves her palms over the fire. The flames turn purple and the image of Lady Madsen appears. Andi recognizes her from the portrait hanging in the Old Main library. Emelie announces, "The former High Priestess welcomes you to our coven. Your training has just begun. As you know the Ancient Library is the repository for all of our knowledge, culture and history. You will find ancient books and scrolls there. The language they are written in comes from our own alphabet. It is a white witch's alphabet. Use the letters of this alphabet to read the text. Study hard and prepare yourself. I and other trusted witches in our coven are your mentors. Remember, Knowledge is Power. Your knowledge of the craft will give you more power. The former High Priestess will communicate with you through premonition, dreams and meditation. One of your biggest weapons are these psychic abilities. With practice, you can pick up others thoughts and send your thoughts into other's minds.

Sending telepathic messages will make others believe these thoughts are a product of their own thinking." Lady Madsen's image fades. The purple flames disappear.

"Her image can only last for a certain amount of time. She is in the spiritual world. She can only straddle the two worlds for a finite period of time. Lady Madsen or Gertrude Madsen is the latest former High Priestess. Her image is the spirit of all previous High Priestess' taking her form, but she appears as she was while she was living. The position of the High Priestess is a lifetime engagement. Once selected, service is for life, and as you have just seen, even into the afterlife."

I ask, "How do we get into the Ancient Library?" Emelie responds, "The secret code is 108801." "Is there any significance to this combination?" Emelie answers, "Yes, first of all, 108801 is the mirror image of 108. 108 holds meaning in various cultures. In Eastern religions, 1 symbolizes the Goddess or the higher truth. 0 symbolizes spiritual completeness and 8 represents infinity or eternity. Another interpretation, is that this number symbolizes time, energy and gravity which are the three possibilities of creation. Whereas, in science this number has special significance, as well. For example, the internal angles of a pentagram are 108 degrees. The diameter of the sun multiplied by 108, equals the distance between the sun and earth. The diameter of the moon multiplied by 108, equals the distance between the earth and moon. There are many more references to this number throughout history. Anyhow, this sacred number seems fitting for the safekeeping of our sacred history."

Chapter 10

The Tablet with Tandori in the Library

We return to the dorms to get ready for tonight's recon mission. I sneak away from the others and head toward the main campus. I feel compelled to keep walking even though I'm not sure where I'm going. I try to clear my head but I have so many questions. I feel unprepared for my new role. I walk past the old growth trees and up the long flight of stairs. I stand at the door, staring through the glass into Old Main. I feel like kicking myself as it dawns on me that I have the combination to the Ancient Library but no way to get into Old Main. I sit on the stairs trying to think of a way to get into the building. Out of frustration, I close my eyes and think hard. Suddenly a thought intrudes into my consciousness, breaking my concentration. I stand up to examine a small window to the left of the door. I take my hand and push it inward, as the intrusive thought directed. The window becomes ajar. I reach inside at an angle then turn the deadbolt on the other side of the door. I step into the building and head for the library. I smile as I look up at the painting of Lady Madsen on the wall. I feel as if I know her. The darkness of the library makes her look more regal and mysterious. I walk over to the side door and push on it. It does not open. I guess Edward did fix it. I enter 108801. The door opens smoothly. I shut it tightly behind me to make sure it is secure. I feel relieved that I don't have to worry about Odious showing up since the combination has been changed and the door fixed. I'm careful not to turn on any lights, so I don't disclose my presence. However, the Ancient Library is deep inside Old Main, like a catacomb. It would be unlikely anyone would notice the lights anyway.

I use my cell phone's flashlight to find my way to the ancient archives. Using one hand to hold the cell phone, I pick out several books and scrolls from the tall shelves with the other hand. I sit down on the stone floor. It's cold and hard. I feel nervous and shaky but try to push these feelings out of my mind. I am more interested in deciphering the writings rather than attending to my anxiety. There I sit, by myself, in the dark, with a small beam of light illuminating the papyrus. A tall stack of books and numerous scrolls lay next to me. I study an unfamiliar alphabet and try to translate the writing in front of me. I recognize the scroll as the one that caught my eye yesterday.

The writing is made up of symbols that are put together to form sentences, like our Latin rooted alphabet. I can't figure out whether this alphabet is phonetic like our alphabet or not. I feel like I'm trying to translate hieroglyphs from the ancient Egyptians without any clue as to where to start. I search various sections of the book for clues.

I point my cell flashlight back toward the shelves. I see a large, square stone tablet that I had not noticed before. It has similar unfamiliar symbols chiseled into it. I become curious and pick it up. As I do this, I see a flash of light and feel overcome. Suddenly large volumes of knowledge download into my head. The symbols on the stone tablet appear inside my head. I fall backward as if struck by a large object or a bolt of lightning. I feel like I'm about to vomit. I lay still trying to breathe deeply in order to shake it off. I feel a profound sense of fatigue.

Once my head had stopped spinning and I was able to sit up again, I notice that the unfamiliar symbols read as if written in English. I examine a book titled "The Witches Book of Knowledge." A bolt of electricity runs down my spine. I try to focus but my concentration shifts to the sensation of the cold, damp and dark room. It feels like a tomb. My heart starts racing and I can't catch my breath. I command my mind to relax and tell myself to breathe deeply. I can feel the power of the book in my hands. It is the repository of our knowledge, culture and history. My hands become warm where I am holding the book. I read on.

The book describes the difference between the physical world on earth and the spiritual world of the dead. It says that spirits come to the physical world to experience life on the physical plane to include bodily sensations and emotions. For example, childbirth, falling in love, dancing, aging, grief, etc. In the physical world, the spirit bonds with the physical body to work with the physical elements. As a result, creations, such as art, literature and architecture are created. In the spiritual world, there is creation but it is only on the spirit level. There is no physical way to interact or physical sensations, as on earth. There is no physical sensation of love, pain or any way to physically manipulate one's environment. On earth, there is a profound presence of good and evil. In the spiritual world, where most of us go after we die, there is no blatant evil. Spirits that are blatantly evil, go to another plane that is reserved for a very small percent of those who align with the very dark forces. Soon thereafter, they are kicked back into the physical world of earth again.

I flip through the pages of the book and my eye catches a chapter titled "Communicating with those in the Spiritual World." I excitedly read on:

"Those who attune to the wavelength of the dead in the spiritual world can communicate with them. The dead want to speak with the living but cannot communicate easily because of the barrier between the spiritual and physical worlds. During certain periods, space and time can be manipulated or reversed to gain access to the different worlds. The dead often want to communicate with those they were connected to during their physical lifespan. They may have a relative, soul mate or animal helper they want to communicate with. Those who were connected at one point in the physical world, form a spiritual bond. Often times this bond is established on earth, on a conscious level. This means that both parties voluntarily agree to become bonded together in a spiritual configuration that is eternal and continues after death. Death does not break this bond. Life and death are a continuum. Energy exists, it just exists in different forms. Sometimes it takes the physical form, sometimes a spiritual form. We are eternal beings because our spirit never dies."

I think back to my physics class in college. $E=mc2$, Einstein's Theory of Special Relativity. This describes the equilibrium between mass and energy. Mass can change from a physical form to energy and back again. The amount of energy and mass are always the same but their form can change between the two.

I flip to another chapter and start reading. This chapter describes how the body, including the brain, is constantly recording. The cells throughout the body and brain hold positive and negatively charged ions within their cells. This is why when we die, we see our life flash before us. When we die our brain and body are actively downloading all of its contents to "The Powers that Be." "The Powers that Be" is a warehouse for knowledge and energy. It is the collective unconscious, or archives of humankind. This is the origins of the archetypes of the world. "The Powers that Be" are accessible to all who have learned to tune into these forces. "The Powers that Be" are a source of knowledge and physical power. The wavelength of "The Powers that Be" is at a different frequency than the power of the dark forces though they are associated.

Again, I think back to the valuable knowledge I learned in college. I see the resemblance of the cells in the body, how they store memory and the way computers store data. Both store memory and data in a similar fashion. I have kept up to date on research in science since college. I recently came across a theory of the Zero Point Energy Field. This is an energy field in the space outside of our bodies and in the actual space of the universe. I wonder if this is science's explanation of the "The Powers that Be", the underpinnings of the collective unconsciousness, a higher power or even the power of magic?

I flip to another chapter and start reading:

"The spiritual world is a sister world or twin world of the physical world on earth. It balances the physical world of earth, with its opposite, the spiritual world. These worlds live next to each other or even on top of each other but they remain separate. The laws of the spiritual world are opposite to the physical laws of earth. The spiritual world is not physical but mimics the appearance of the physical world on earth. The substance of this spiritual world is only energy, not physical mass. For example, in the spiritual world, aging is reversed. On earth, physical beings go through a physical and linear process of aging. As they age their immune system and physical body degenerates until they die from a physical illness or injury, such as cardiovascular disease, cancer or another opportunistic disease or a fall, accident etc.

They then transition to the spiritual world where they age backwards from older to younger. They heal from what caused their physical death and continue aging backwards until they are fully healed and healthy. They generally stay at a certain age for a while but eventually continue aging backwards until they transition into a fetus. Once this happens, they are born again into the physical world as a baby. Then the aging process is reversed and they get older and continue the cycle of life all over again. This is a cyclical event from one world to another.

The spiritual world is a mirror image of earth, so the seasons are reversed, direction is reversed, etc. So, when it is summer in the physical world, it is winter in the spiritual world."

I look down at my cell phone and notice it's getting late and my phone needs recharging. I don't want it to die while I'm in the darkness of the library. As I look up again, I question whether I'm groggy from my experience or I am seeing a beam of light coming out of the darkness. I listen in the stillness. I think I hear footsteps. Is it my imagination? I panic remembering that Odious had transgressed on the Ancient Library before. I stand up, though I feel weak and unstable. I flatten my body against the wall trying to hide. I look for an object to defend myself. I grab a book that appears to be titled "The Witches Book of the Dead." There is nothing else to grab in the instance. I see the beam of light getting bolder and hear the footsteps getting louder. I grip the book tightly in a sacrilegious way, pulling it back to gain momentum for impact. My heart is pounding and I almost pass out from holding my breath. I jump around the corner. A flashlight falls to the ground. I stand staring face to face with a person that I cannot see in the darkness. My eyes acclimate. I see a woman dressed in a dark uniform. "Officer Tandori? I almost hit you with this book." Shamita replies, "I almost shot you with my gun." Shamita then exclaims, "I almost got killed by The Witches Book of the Dead? How ironic!" After hearing this, I stare at her in silence. I know that an ordinary person would not know the name of a title written in the Witch's Alphabet or the combination to get into the Ancient Library. Shamita winks at me and says "I'm good friends with Emilie." Shamita has obviously outed herself. "What are you doing here Andi?" "Oh, just doing some research. I'm writing a book and Emelie gave me permission to use this library." "Oh, okay, then I guess I will not arrest you." I laugh but am still guarded as Emelie mentioned that she is unsure who to trust in the coven. I announce, "I think I'll be going now. I got what I needed and it's time for dinner." Officer Tandori agrees "Yes, it is getting late. I will walk you out."

I follow Shamita out. In order to make small talk, I mention that I was once an officer. Shamita turns around to look at me but keeps walking at a slower pace. "Yeah" I say. "The job is not for everyone in the long-term. I became very disillusioned with law enforcement. Especially the para-militaristic hierarchy and the politics. I was initially excited to have a female Sergeant in a male dominated occupation but I soon realized that she held every negative stereotype associated with being a female, being a boss and a cop. She was especially critical of the female officers. We already have a tough time working in a male dominated environment without any added stressors. My Sergeant deluded the higher brass to believe she was competent."

"One night she was called to the field. It was a Domestic Violence call where a man had barricaded himself, his girlfriend and their five-year old daughter in their home. We surround the home. He had been drinking and was convinced his girlfriend had been cheating on him. He had prior arrests for DV charges. We were waiting for the Negotiator and SWAT to arrive, so we just sat on containment. My Sergeant engages the suspect in a verbal exchange over the phone. She challenges him, saying he is worthless and not man enough to fight off the SWAT team. Of course, he is drunk and not perceiving or interpreting things well. As you know, when people drink their judgment and impulse control becomes impaired. So, my Sergeant continues to pick at the suspect. She tells him that he may as well put down the gun and come out because everyone knows he doesn't have the balls to use it. My Sergeant then orders me to enter the home. I look at her puzzled as the Negotiator and SWAT are in route. She orders me again, so I kick the door open. When the suspect sees me, he points his gun at me. We stand there staring at each other with our guns pointed at each other. Suddenly he turns toward his girlfriend who is holding their five-year-old. The mother was trying protect and calm the child. The suspect raises his gun to her head and proceeds to shoot her. She crumples and falls away from the little girl. There is blood and brain splatter all over the child. The child is screaming and crying hysterically. Then the suspect turns back toward me, directing his gun at me again. At this point, I have no other option than to shoot him. The suspect basically defers to the old "suicide by cop" method of suicide. So, the little girl ends up witnessing both her mother and father's death that night. In the end, my Sergeant denied ordering me to enter the home before the Negotiator and SWAT arrive. I get written-up and placed on probation. My career is ruined. Since then, every night before I go to sleep, when I shut my eyes, I see this little girl's face as she witnesses both her parents die. This experience has forever changed me. Of course, my Sergeant is promoted to Captain. She was able to deflect any criticism directed at her and redirect it toward me. I resign shortly thereafter and become a private investigator."

Shamita puts her hand on my shoulder to comfort me. She opens the door, so I can exit the building then closes it behind me. She retreats back into the building.

Shamita returns to the Ancient Library. She picks up the book that Andi was getting ready to hit her with. She shelves "The Witches Book of the Dead", sliding it tightly into the shelf. This caused another book fall out the back of the shelf. Shamita bends down to pick it up. She reads the title, "The Command of Fire." She opens the book to see Gertrude Madsen's name written on the inside cover. She thinks back to her upbringing as a Parsi. A religion that is not well known in the United States. This religion uses fire in their temples and sees it as a sacred symbol. She thinks how her former religious beliefs prepared her to become a witch. There are similarities between the two. Unfortunately, Sid has taken the element of fire and used it in a perverse way. Thankfully Lady Madsen always used fire for the good. Out of habit Shamita reaches down to feel her Sudrah underneath her uniform shirt. She makes sure the Kutsi cord is tied properly. She ritualistically whispers the tenets of her former religion, "Good words, good thoughts and good deeds." She does not see any problem with combining the two religions since they complement each other. She laughs to herself wondering how her mother, Soonu would feel about this thought process. She would probably approve of it more than her choice of becoming a cop. It's not that mom is closed minded but she does worry about my safety. Shamita states her craft name quietly to herself, "Ahura."

I arrive at the Safehaven dorms and notice my door is open. Harley, Lexa, Juni and Lawren are having a potluck inside the dorm with a menagerie of mismatched food that they communally donated. A makeshift meal as the cafeteria is closed since the reunion is technically over. Sam is lying on my bed. She looks up with her big yellow eyes, making my heart melt. I take out my hummus, vegetables and remaining Zinfandel from the fridge. Harley says "Sam has been crying ever since you left." I pick her up and squeeze her as if I would never let her go. She purrs loudly and licks my chin. I breathe in the fresh smell of her fur and new cat breath.

We sit on the beds enjoying our food and wine. Lawren appears to be taking pleasure in our company. I wonder how we are going to ditch her again tonight, so we can go to the steam sculpture to gain intelligence on the Darksiders. She is on her third glass of wine and is laughing and engaging with the others. I wink at Lexa indicating

it is time to head out. She makes up an excuse about needing to meet Emelie at the main campus. Lawren misses the cue in her drunken state and asks to go with. Lexa suggests that Lawren may want to stay at the dorm to sober up. Lawren rebuffs this notion and walks over to Lexa and gives her a big, friendly hug. Lexa looks uncomfortable and makes a shrugging gesture indicating she has done her best to get rid of Lawren. Lawren slurs her words as she talks about how she initially thought we didn't like her because we were always trying to get rid of her but she knows better now. Harley steps in and guides her to her dorm room. Lawren grabs my full glass of wine on her way and takes several big gulps. She holds the glass of wine tightly to her chest so it won't be taken away. She sits on her bed, then lays back. She quickly falls asleep. We look at each other gleefully and hurry to the door. Harley quietly shuts the door.

We gather at the pond in front of the Safehaven dorms. There are rocks that border the outer edge of the pond. We sit on the rocks and join hands. I lead a meditation. I close my eyes to calm my mind and body. I request guidance and assistance for our mission. I feel a wave of relaxation come over me. My mind becomes silent and I feel like I'm on the edge of sleep. In my mind's eye, I see the image of Lady Madsen. She smiles lovingly. I hear the words "black rock." Her image fades but I remain in a state of relaxation. Slowly I start to come out of my altered state of consciousness but I'm still unable to open my eyes. This sensation feels so good that I want to remain in this state forever but feel myself being thrust back into alertness. My head jerks forward and my eyes open wide. The others are conscious already and waiting for me. They ask "What did you see?" I tell them the word "black rock." Lexa asks, "What does that mean?" I say "I don't know. Did any of you get any messages or images?" The other three look at each other. Juni says, "I saw a doll that is vaguely familiar to me but I can't place where I've seen it before." Harley said "I saw an image of a beautiful bird frozen in flight." Lexa said, "I saw the flames of a fire." She stares off into the distance, then quietly announces, "Fire scares me" then grabs at her stomach. I ask her, "Cramping again, Lexa?" "Yeah, I hope I can get through this without having to make an emergency stop."

I stand and announce, "It is time to head out." Lexa looks apprehensive. Juni and Harley are still holding her hand from the meditation. They tug at her simultaneously, pulling her up off the rock. We walk together in the direction of the main campus and the steam sculpture. On the way, we discuss our tactics such as how to surround and spy on the pack without being noticed. We decide to split up. I go in the direction of north, Juni goes south, Lexa goes east and Harley goes west.

As I approach my post, I see that the Darksiders are already there. The sculpture's bed of rock is discharging a significant amount of steam. I can see the flames from pocket lighters, light up and go out, through the steam. I can see the glow of something burning and smell an offensive odor. I recognize it from my police days as stimulant drugs. These types of drugs make people physically strong, unpredictable and irrational. I stand at the nearest building for cover. I will wait here for a while until I can approach the sculpture without being seen. Thankfully I have a black coat and hat on making it harder to be seen in the dark. I see Lexa to the left of me, Harley, on the right, but Juni is not in sight. I am nervous the others may be detected as they do not have the stealth training that I received in the police department. I motion for Lexa and Harley to stay put. I make my move toward the sculpture but jump back into hiding when I realize someone is walking up the brick walkway. The figure is walking slow, teetering from side to side and seems to lack direction. I squint to see in the dark. I say to myself, "Oh, no! It can't be!" There is Lawren walking my way. She is obviously intoxicated and vulnerable. I relinquish my position and walk toward her trying to intercept her. Abruptly she takes a turn and heads toward the steam sculpture. My heart skips several beats. She has yards to go before reaching the sculpture. I rush over, grab her, trying to divert her into another direction. She laughs loudly. "Andi, there you are. I thought you were meeting Emelie?" I hear the conversation amongst the Darksiders cease.

I turn and pull Lawren away from the sculpture. She falls limp in my arms, to the ground then stiffens up. The sculpture has dim lights that are used to accentuate its' artistic qualities. As the steam rises, the light is captured in the droplets of the steam and refracted in an unusual way. This effect attracts Lawren in her drunken state. The smell of drugs concentrates and sits in the dense air. A dark figure emerges from the steam. It appears to be Odious. He does not seem to recognize me. I explain, in a disguised voice, that my friend is drunk and won't remember a thing in the morning. He looks angry. I pull at Lawren but she pulls away from me. Odious raises his hand and a small bolt of energy is directed our way. It hits us and we fall down. Lawren starts to scream in pain. I feel a scorching energy run through my body, down my legs and into the ground. Pain chases the electricity. I'm immobilized. I can't get up from the ground. Odious heads toward us with his palms pointed outward. I grip for another bolt. Instantly, Odious is distracted and turns away, heading off in another direction. After several minutes, I am able to move again. I gather Lawren and carry her back to the dorm to put her to bed.

Lexa and Harley rush into Lawren's room through the shared bathroom. Harley shouts, "What happened? What was that flash of light? Are you okay?" I assure them I'm alright. "Lawren was stumbling across campus in a drunken state and drew their attention. I tried to grab her to quiet her. Odious struck us with a bolt of energy from his palms. This bolt knocked both of us to the ground. Afterwards I was able to carry Lawren back but she does not seem to be alert. I can't get her attention. I even tried slapping her face. Now she appears to be sleeping." I glance over periodically to make sure her chest is expanding and contracting to confirm she is breathing. "I thought Odious was going to finish us off. He was walking toward us as if he were going to attack again then abruptly turned away. Where is Juni?" Lexa and Harley look at each other. "We don't know." I jump up in concern and head toward the door. Just then Juni appears. "Thank Goddess you are safe!" Juni smiles. She seems proud of herself. "Yeah, I saw what happened. Remember I have a background in entertainment. Once I played a role as a ventriloquist. I saw Odious walking toward you and Lawren, ready to strike again. So, I threw my voice, imitating, Sid. He appears to be their leader and Odious seems afraid of him. That is all I could think of to do. Thankfully, it worked. I was able to get close enough to hear what they were talking about. First of all, Nefara is a slut. After flirting with me all afternoon, she was all over Odious at the steam sculpture. She doesn't hold her drugs well either. Anyway, I heard them say they are going to plant a mole in our coven that will report back to them."

I sit contemplating Juni's words when I hear a familiar howl. "Emilie must be here." We run back into our dorm room, closing the door quietly to the adjoining bathroom, not to wake Lawren. Emelie is already inside our room. She tells us she knows what happened and congratulates us on our first official mission. She winks at Juni as she speaks.

Emelie invites us to the ash spreading ceremony of the former High Priestess tomorrow evening. She reinforces that this is a highly sensitive and sacred ceremony. We all shake our heads in understanding. Emelie continues, "Lady Madsen died under suspicious circumstances. It was a fire. Gertrude was a master of commanding the flames. We think she was murdered. The Darksiders are our prime suspects. Though the police were involved, it is a cold case. The witches want someone held responsible. Sid is Gertrude's son. She was very disappointed with him when he revolted and formed the Darksiders. When one partakes in the dark energy, the dark energy takes them. This is what happened to Sid. As he entertained the dark side, he became darker. Eventually he turned his back on his family and friends. He became obsessed with power and money. Lady Madsen tried to talk to him to no avail. Being dark is a choice. As he continued to make dark choices, he spiraled further and further into the darkness. His judgment and insight became affected as he lost his connection to the light. He became intoxicated by, and addicted to, the power and the money that comes with dark energy. Once indulged, it is hard to give up. The white witches are working on a treatment program to reform anyone wanting to return to our coven. They first must voluntarily denounce the dark and accept the light. The treatment isn't effective yet but the idea is to change the frequency in which they fluctuate. It's called entrainment but basically this means getting all the energy to synchronize and harmonize in a positive direction. Though, I am not sure Sid could ever rehabilitate."

Emelie changes the subject, "I brought some gifts for you girls." Emelie takes out four necklaces. All of them are made of the same material but each is original in content, size and shape. "My dears, these are amber necklaces. They are rare resins made from a tree. Amber is rare in itself but especially when it comes from an ancient and sacred pear tree. This amber is from The Tree of Life. It has healing and protective qualities. I think these gifts are very fitting after what happened tonight." Emelie holds a necklace up to the light. The light outlines an object in the middle of the amber. "Amber is sticky and typically, there are insects, small animals or plant life around the tree where it accumulates. As a consequence, these types of things stick to the amber and the amber continues to build around it, encapsulating the object inside. This is a chrysalis cocoon. It is the resting and transitory stage for a caterpillar before it turns into a beautiful butterfly. It symbolizes transformation." Emelie places the necklace around my neck. She holds another necklace up in the light. "This is a Dragonfly." She places the necklace around Harley's neck and carefully latches the clasp. "Dragonflies symbolize change and self-realization, wisdom and adaptability. Besides they are very exciting insects to watch as they gracefully fly then abruptly change direction in mid-air." Emelie takes out another necklace. There is a bright red Ladybug preserved in its center. Lexa looks eager to get this necklace but Emelie places it on Juni's neck. "The Ladybug or Lady Beetle as it is now appropriately called, is a symbol of luck. Every gardener is happy to see these in their garden." "Lastly", Emelie takes out the last necklace with a small bee in the amber. Emelie announces, "Bees symbolize unity, family ties and hard work." She places it around Lexa's neck. Lexa seems just as happy to get this necklace. "All these little animals once lived on or around The Tree of Life. They were part of the tree's ecosystem." All four of us stand proudly displaying our new necklaces.

"How are your meditations going? Are you becoming more sensitive and intuitive? This will come." There is a sound of a fox in the background. "I need to leave now. Oh, and the amber also protects against attacks of negative psychic energies. Remember to wear your amber and practice your protection spell. It seems the Darksiders now know about you. You must always be on guard and ready to protect yourself." She disappears from the room.

Chapter 11

A Familiar Feeling

I toss and turn all night. I see the images I saw when I touched the stone tablet earlier today. This continues all night during a semi- sleep-like state. My mind goes over and over this knowledge. Spells unfold, symbols dance and I see movies play out that show me the history of the witches of Safehaven. I see bits of images from more ancient times but I don't quite understand them. I see images of fire. I wake, wet with sweat and torment. Then, I drift in and out of sleep for the rest of the night.

In the morning, I wake fatigued from the night. Harley is sitting on my bed. The morning light hurts my eyes as I look up at her. The sensation of wanting to vomit crawls up my throat. I jump up and run to the bathroom. I'm not sure which end it will come out. I lose my bowels just as I reach the toilet. I think to myself that this is a replay from yesterday. At least the diarrhea took away the nausea. Harley is still sitting on my bed when I return to the room. Harley asks, "Are you okay? You were tossing and turning all night. Your sheets are soaking wet with sweat." I say "I know. It was a rough night." I didn't want to tell her about the stone tablet. "Where is Lawren?" "I don't know. It's been quiet in her room all morning." I walk through the shared bathroom to her dorm room. Harley follows. I knock on the door. There is no answer. I slowly turn the doorknob, opening the door slightly to look in. I see Lawren sleeping quietly. I hesitate but decide to enter her room. I sit on her bed. Her curly brown hair forms big, complete ringlets that fall upon her face. Her eyelids flutter as she slowly opens her big green eyes. "Good morning Lawren. How are you feeling?" She sits up and stretches, raising her arms high in the air. "I feel great" she says. "I must have drunk way too much at dinner. I don't remember anything that happened last night." I look at Harley in surprise. I turn back to Lawren. "Yeah, after dinner you laid down and slept all night." "Well, I feel rested, except my skin feels tingly, like I got a sunburn." I casually look over to Lawren's desk and see an empty baggie that had held the tea with the word "Memory" in Edward's handwriting.

"We are going to go back to our dorm to get ready for breakfast." I pull Harley by the hand out into the hallway and push her into Juni's and Lexa's door. I knock quietly but in a fast, excited tempo. I don't want Lawren to hear me. Lexa opens the door and I push Harley through the doorway, almost knocking Lexa down. I tell Lexa and Juni about giving Lawren the tea yesterday and how nervous I was that Lawren witnessed witchcraft last night. I tell them that Lawren has no memory of the events last night. "It worked! Edward's tea worked. Lawren lost her memory after she drank the Memory Tea. We don't need to give any explanation or come out to her. I am relieved because I didn't know how I was going handle it." Lexa asks, "She literally has no memory at all? I think I need some of that tea. I could forget my ex and all the embarrassing moments in my life. Or better yet, give it to the people who witnessed me in these moments. Hey, I wonder if Edward has a tea that replaces their memories of my embarrassing moments with memories of me being perfect? I will have to ask him." Lexa continues to ramble, "Why don't we go to the Biodynamic Farm for breakfast? I can see Susy. I wish my animal helper could fit in my shirt, like Sam." I look down at Sam, who is rubbing against my leg. I scoop her up, hug her tightly then guide her into my shirt. She lets out a deep, coarse happy-purr.

Edward is at the pharm. He is cooking over the fire. Emelie is sitting near him drinking coffee that has percolated over the fire. Emelie greets us. "I spoke with Shamita earlier today. She told me that the Darksiders left the steam sculpture a mess. There was evidence of witchcraft. They left burned candles, unusual symbols drawn with a red substance and remnants of drug use. Not to mention vandalism. The university administration is very concerned and afraid this will affect its new student enrollment. Andi, a witness saw you at the steam sculpture last night and recognized you as a Safehaven alumni. Safehaven is coming under scrutiny. It is a modern-day witch hunt. We have to divert attention away from Safehaven. Of course, the white witches have friends amongst the administrators. They don't know who reported you."

There is a buzzing noise overhead. I look up to see a beautifully marked humming bird hovering in the air and looking our way in curiosity. Lexa says "There's been a humming bird flying around your dorm window all morning." The bird seems to fly at the speed of sound. It flies around Harley's head then disappears. Harley says, "Yeah, I had one follow me across campus yesterday....." She stops in the middle of her next sentence and appears deep in thought. "It looked just like this one with those unusual markings." We all look at her. "Congratulations Harley. I think your animal helper has found you", "They can fly sixty-three miles per hour but they appear to fly faster." Lexa says, "It's because you are so sweet. Just like nectar." "They are certainly masters of flight. Very useful qualities for a familiar", Emelie comments. I ask, "Do the Darksiders have familiars?" Emelie responds, "No. They are not connected to nature as we are. Occasionally they mingle with animals but only brief interactions." I swallow hard, as if there is a big lump in my throat. "Emelie, the Darksiders are sending a mole to spy on us. What if Sam or one of the other animal helpers are actually a mole?" I set Sam on the ground and continue, "Certainly the use of a black cat is symbolic. It would break my heart if it's Sam." "The Darksiders feed off this type of energy. Energy caused by betrayal, violence, drug use or any other type of wrong doing, in general. It gives them energy. At this time, trust no one, including your familiars."

I change the subject. "Emelie, do you know anything about the stone tablet in the Ancient Library? I picked it up and had a very unusual experience." Emelie stares at me but didn't seem especially surprised. I continue, "It was as if a large amount of information was being downloaded into my brain but I don't understand it. It swirls around in my head, especially while I am sleeping, but it doesn't make any sense. I see symbols flash in my mind but I don't know their meaning." In a sincere manner, Emelie explains. "Not everyone who touches the tablet gets this information. Only those who are special have this experience. These symbols are our antiquity. The use of these symbols over centuries by our ancestors gives them power. So, when you use a symbol, you don't have to focus as much energy on intent. This has already been done for you by centuries of practice. This is why people practice ritual. These rituals become entrenched. It's similar to your nervous system. Activities you engage in regularly are more deeply entrenched in your nervous system and become

Lawrence Anderson

habits. You don't even have to think about them. The pathways are etched, like a well-used path in your brain. This is the same for spells, symbols and rituals that have been practiced throughout history. The more you use them, the easier they are accessed and the more powerful they are. Andi, you must go through a ceremony and be anointed before you can have access to the meaning of this information. It is downloaded, like a computer but you don't have an icon to access it. We can do an anointment at the ash spreading ceremony tonight. Are you able to read using the Witches Alphabet?" I nod apprehensively, as if I have been caught stealing a cookie out of the cookie jar. Emelie smiles with pride.

Edward points into the bushes. We all look but don't see anything. I continue to focus in this direction and after a while, I see subtle movement in the brush. I focus for a few more minutes, trying to decipher what caused the movement. Slowly, a young fawn colored deer steps out of the foliage. She is a light brown color with a black tail. Edward tells us the doe has been hanging around the Biodynamic Farm for the last day. Juni gets up and walks toward it.

She rips off a leaf from a tree as she walks. The deer does not flee. Juni holds out the leaf. The deer slowly lowers her head and nibbles at

94

the leaf in her hand. Juni carefully rubs the deer's forehead. The doe remains still and closes her eyes in pleasure. Juni is thrilled to finally meet her familiar. The deer leans into Juni and rests her head on her arm. As she returns to the campfire, the deer follows. The doe wags her black tail enthusiastically, like a dog. We sit near the fire with all our animal helpers next to us in a circle. We are one big family.

Chapter 12

Fate at SMT

It was several hours before my anointing and the ash spreading ceremony. I notice I misplaced my overshirt. The last time I remember wearing it was on the tour of the Biology Department. I walk across campus toward SMT. This is one of my favorite shirts. I would be devastated if I lost it. I like it even more since I can easily conceal Sam inside.

I can't bear to think Sam may be the mole and I may not be able to trust her. This is why I left her sitting on my bed in the dorm, but I already miss her. I'm preoccupied with this thought as I enter the building and take the stairs down to the basement. As I approach room B-66, I hear the crashing of glass breaking. I look up and focus. Dr. Slater and Sid are in the lab, facing away from me. Across the room stands Dr. Santiago with a significant amount of space between her and the other two. Sid is angry and yelling at her. He suspects Dr. Santiago has something to do with the missing High Priestess' ashes. I stand frozen trying to understand what is taking place. He raises his hand with his palm extended. He casts an energy bolt toward Dr. Santiago but misses her as she ducks. The bolt hits a beaker sitting on the lab bench next to her. It shatters into hundreds of pieces and falls to the floor. Dr. Santiago is clearly fearful for her life. She continues to crouch behind the lab bench. Dr. Slater refers to her as "Blanca" in a derogatory fashion. I remember this is the Spanish word for white and the word that came to me during a meditation.

I act instinctually and step into the room just before Sid gets ready to finish her off with a succession of bolts. Sid sees me and turns his attention and rage toward me. He readies himself to send a

bolt my way. At this moment, Harley, Lexa and Juni enter the lab. Sid is interrupted one more time and stops to notice my friends. They run toward me and grab my hand. I can hear all three chanting to initiate the Protection Spell. We encircle Dr. Santiago, bringing her into the center of the circle for protection. I quickly ask Harley how did you know I needed help. She quickly replies that our powers seem to be getting stronger. They sensed I needed help and knew where to find me. "We dropped everything and came running." Feeling grateful, I grasp my amber necklace and recite the Protection Spell.

Sid throws a fiery bolt our way. The Protection Spell holds off the bolt like a force field. Its energy disperses and branches out into small fingers of lightning. I can feel that Sid is a powerful witch. A weak spot has started to develop in the force field where the bolt struck. I focus my attention, imagining the weak spot filling in and becoming stronger. Sid's second blow interrupts my concentration. I feel overpowered by his force. I open my eyes to see the force field thin out again. I feel a small jolt of energy hit my body as it breaks through our force field. I close my eyes again and call out for help, loudly in my mind. Dr. Santiago screams in pain as the bolt hits her. I think of my mother then my sister and hope I will see them soon. I feel resignation and acceptance of what is happening. I think of my children.

I'm distracted from my internal dialogue by a noise across the room in the entryway of the lab. I open my eyes to see Emelie move across the room at the speed of light. She waves her arms frantically producing a watery gel in the air. The gel resembles water that has been encapsulated. It forms a wall in front of us. Sid scoffs, "Nice to see you, sister. If mom and dad were alive there would be someone here to miss you." He directs a powerful pulse of energy toward her. Emelie deflects the bolt and retorts, "If mom and dad were alive, they would be very disappointed in you." Sid continues, "You were always their perfect child." Emelie adds, "You were always the one who took the easy way out. Never wanting to take time to do the right thing." Sid replies, "There is one thing I will to do right." The bolt directed at her has increased strength. Emelie deflects the bolt again and interjects, "I have mom's ashes now. You will never learn her secrets or the secrets of our coven. It is over now, Obsidian."

Dr. Slater walks toward Emelie in menacing way. Edward enters the lab and throws something that looks like herbs into the room. Emelie raises her hands and says a prayer asking for the

assistance from the former High Priestess and all of our ancestors. The encapsulated wall of water breaks falling onto a lightning bolt. The water conducts the electricity from the bolt and redirects it back toward Sid. Dr. Slater stops in his tracks, hesitates, then runs towards the door. Emelie chants a time/space spell. Sid and Dr. Slater disappear. The circle's force field runs out of energy, dissipates and disappears. The floor is dry.

Chapter 13

Dr. Slater

Sid and Dr. Slater look around. They are standing in the lab alone. There is no evidence of a battle. A beaker is on the work bench, not shattered into pieces on the floor. "What time is it?" Dr. Slater looks at his watch. "It is 9:05 a.m. on Sunday, June 23rd." Sid does a double fist pump and yells "Yeah! We beat them at their own game." He walks quickly to the specimen storage area. He puts in the combination and the drawer opens. He reaches inside and takes out the ashes of the late High Priestess. "We went back in time. Before the ashes were stolen back." He holds the ashes close to his chest. "We have to analyze these ashes quickly. Can you read the genetic code today?" Dr. Slater shuffles in place then smiles taking the sample. He doesn't mention that Luciana is the one who has the expertise in this area. He dilutes the sample by putting it into solution. He walks over to the Ultra Performance Liquid Chromatograph and injects it into the instrument using a syringe.

Dr. Eric Slater was not the most gifted scientist. His father was the one who wanted him to be a scientist. His father told him genetics would be the future of science. All causes of disease would be revealed and treated through the practice of genetics. He would never have to worry about supporting his family. Eric was always trying to please his father. Somehow, he always fell short. He would've flunked out of college had his father not been able to intervene and make a financial contribution to the school. The four-year program took Eric over six years to complete. Eric was able to network with some professors and do an internship at a pharmaceutical company to complete his Bachelor's Degree. This along with his father's financial support, allowed him to get into a private university for his doctorate program. Luckily, he met Luciana in his first year of this program.

Eric was able to pair up with Luciana for studying, work-groups and labs. Their thesis projects were complementary, so they were able to do their research together. She was the brainstorm. Luciana didn't mind the long hours in the library and lab. She didn't seem to miss the nights out with friends or dating during the academic year. Eric knew she would always pick up his slack. Luciana would update him on whatever he needed to know. Eric was able to listen then skillfully regurgitate what Luciana told him as if he understood it.

Luciana was offered a professorship at Wasgard. She was their first pick. After she took the position, she created another position for Eric in the department. They continued to be a team, just like graduate school. She was the brains and Eric, the brawn. He networked, showed up at fundraisers and attended meetings with the department heads. Luciana liked being in the background. Eric would free her up to do the real work. After all, she was better suited for the isolation caused by long hours in the lab. Eric was the one who had the gift of gab.

Eric fumbled with the Ultra Performance Liquid Chromatograph, or UPLC. He had watched Luciana run thousands of samples over the years. She confidently injected the samples either manually or by using the automated pipettes for bulk projects. She was able to run the samples with consistency, interpret the data then utilize the information gathered. This she accomplished with ease. Luciana was brilliant.

Sweat beaded up on Eric's forehead and upper lip. Sid was hovering over him waiting for the data to come out. The monitor displayed preliminary data. Eric thought about his father then thought about how he was going to tell Sid that he can't interpret the data.

The computer prints out the results. The sample is identified as a female, Caucasian, of Northern European ancestry, approximately sixty years old, with blue eyes and fair skin. The printout lists other demographics and reports her genome originated in Africa. After this information, the instrument plots out a two-dimensional configuration of her DNA. Eric remembers that for the samples Luciana ran, additional genetic information was distal to the primary DNA. This information was the epigenetic information that was the result of genetic changes due to lifestyle, culture and learning. Eric examines the nucleotides but they looked like a foreign language. Unfortunately, a language he did not know.

Eric relives being ten-years old again. He is in elementary school on the playground. The taller boys, who were also more athletic and better looking than him, stand around him. They call him a big, stinky, black rock. "E-reek Slate-r. No, you're a big lump of coal." They start throwing rocks at him.

Chapter 14

The Consequences of Magic

"What happened?" I ask. Emelie explains "We outnumbered Sid. We are stronger in numbers. His powers were fading. Then I used the time/space spell. Either Sid and Dr. Slater went forward, or backward in time. I am not sure which."

"Sid's power comes from the element of Fire. It is a destructive force. This is the primary source of power for the Darksiders. Water is life giving and healing. This is one of our sources of power. Water puts out fire. I'm concerned there will be consequences because of our use of strong magic. It disturbs the balance in the world. We have to wait and see if there are any significant consequences." Emelie pats herself in the stomach area. She reaches under her shawl and unties a linen pouch that was secured to her waist. She opens it to confirm what she already suspected. The High Priestess' ashes are no longer in the pouch. Emelie looks up, staring into the distance. "They obviously went back in time. Hurry we must try to intervene before it is too late."

I look over at Dr. Santiago. She is standing stiff and motionless. Her eyes are staring blankly into the distance. She appears to be having trouble assimilating the recent events. "Are you okay Luciana?" She turns with wide eyes. "This must be a dream. I told Dr. Slater I had contacted you this morning after I heard the administration suspected Safehaven had something to do with the vandalism at the steam sculpture last night. I am a fan of Safehaven and wanted to offer my support. This must have made Sid suspicious."

"Why was Dr. Swhart talking about ashes? Are the rumors true? Is there witchcraft on this campus? I thought this was just an urban legend to bring more students to the campus. Why did he call me Blanca? I'm not white. I'm Hispanic." Emelie touches her shoulder lightly. "He meant he believes you're a white witch and you're working with us."

I put my arm around Luciana to give her physical support as we walk back to the Safehaven dorms. I help her down onto a bed in the vacant room connected to Lexa and Juni's dorm. She is shivering, so I cover her with a blanket. "I'm afraid Sid will come back for me. He is so angry. How can I protect myself? He is so powerful." I hold her hand and Emelie rubs her head gently. Luciana says something under her breath, moving her lips only slightly. She speaks in a flat monotone. I ask her to speak up. "Eric cannot read the data. He thinks I don't know this but I do. He doesn't understand our research." I look at Emelie contemplating this news. I ask, "Does this mean our secrets are safe?" Emelie looks at Luciana. Luciana nods her head, "Yes." I let out a sigh.

Emelie has a concerned look on her face. "This is why strong magic is only used as a last resort. These are the consequences. We cannot leave the High Priestess' ashes with Sid and the Darksiders." Edward walks into the room holding a steaming cup of tea and hands it to Luciana. She takes a sip then puts down the cup and closes her eyes. She lets out a muffled snore.

We step away. Edward winks, "My Sleep Tea. She should sleep restfully for a couple of hours." Emelie points out, "This way we can watch her and keep her safe. But be careful, we don't know who is the mole." I add, "Swhart did conveniently miss her with his bolt but in her defense, she did duck quickly." Edward adds, "She is the only one who can read the data. We have to keep her in our care as long as possible. Even if she is the mole." We exit the dorms, heading for the pharm. I am at the head of the pack when I hear a scream. I turn around immediately thinking we are under attack again. I see Lexa laying on the ground. She bellows, "Ouch! Shit! Damn ground hogs." She quickly gets up on both feet, as if getting up from a tumble on the basketball court. "I'm okay. I hate rodents." Lexa limps but stoically tries to walk it off. The group waits for her to rejoin them as they continue to walk to the Learning Center.

The fire crackles and lets off a wet wood smell. Edward hands each of us a cup of tea. He refuses to tell us the kind of tea and waits for our feedback. Lexa blows on the tea, takes a big sip, closes her eyes and sits back in her chair. Suddenly she grimaces and spits out the tea. Harley smells the tea and says, "It's Ginseng?." Edward nods. Lexa loudly adds, "It tastes bad enough. I hope it has pain killing qualities. My ankle hurts." Lexa starts another sentence but is distracted by movement from the ground. She yells, "There is that bastard" as she points. We turn our heads and look where she is pointing. Edward takes a heavy chunk of firewood and throws it violently at a little rodent, who is boring up through the ground. The large piece of wood misses but would have surely killed the little animal. It turns back into its hole and goes underground.

We all turn and stare at Edward in surprise. He is such a gentle man and this behavior is uncharacteristic. "Edward, when did you stop loving little creatures?" exclaims Emelie. Edward turns and looks around the circle as he speaks. "The holes in the ground at the dorms and the pharm are new holes." Emelie acknowledges this by shaking her head up and down. "Yes, but we can fix the holes in the dirt easily enough." Edward continues, "It's a rodent." Emelie continues, "Yes, Edward but a harmless animal." Edward blurts out, "It's a shrew." We look at each other trying to understand the problem. Lexa squints and says "It's not a Groundhog? Sorry, I flunked Taxonomy in college. No offense intended." Edward continues, "The average person would mistake a shrew for a mole. A shrew looks like a mole but has smaller feet and more distinct eyes. They are omnivores instead of carnivores. Moles have pointy noses and large feet. Their eyes and ears are so small they aren't even visible. When you heard that the Darksiders sent out a mole, they literally meant a mole. Unfortunately, they don't know the difference between the two animals. However, a shrew is more fitting for them."

Emelie smiles. "Let me guess. Sid put Odious in charge of this task. I'm glad we found this out before we talked about our strategy to get the High Priestess' ashes back." Edward stands up and leads us down a path into the forest. He stops at the trunk of a large, old growth, evergreen tree. He reaches up and pulls on a rope. A staircase drops down. We climb up the staircase to another staircase that is stationary and built around the large trunk of the tree. It leads to a platform. Edward opens a hatch underneath the platform and we climb up into what appears to be the living room of a tree house. There is a small couch, chairs and a small wood stove with a fire burning in it. The room is warm, comfortable and inviting. There's a small kitchen and bathroom on either side of the living room. Up another ladder is a small bedroom with a view from high in the tree looking down on a lower canopy of trees. "It's safe to talk here. The shrew cannot get up here. Now we are fairly sure our animal helpers aren't the mole and this would also exclude Luciana. Sid and Eric already have the DNA results by now, so the ashes may not be as important as they once were. Hopefully they will be more careless about where they hide the remaining ashes. If we get the ashes back in the next couple hours, we can still have the ash spreading ceremony tonight. I have a plan. Follow me."

I didn't want to leave the tree house since it was so warm and relaxing. We reconvene at the Learning Center. The campfire is still going and the bitter tea is still warm. As we are waiting for Edward to tell us his master plan, we are suddenly bombarded by pieces of organic matter coming up from the earth. In front of our eyes we see an animal tunneling up from below. It busily cuts through the soil with great force but little effort. Edward just sits there. Meanwhile, Lexa and Juni each grab a large piece of firewood readying to throw it at the vermin. Edward holds his hand up in silence. Lexa and Juni set the wood down staring at Edward in disbelief. "This is my friend, Holy. He is truly a mole. I have solicited him to help us. He will go find the Darksiders and will be our mole. Since they don't know the difference between a shrew and a mole, they won't notice he is not the same animal that is working for them." Lexa pipes in "Is his name Holy Moley or Holy Mole'?" She uses different emphasis and giggles to herself. "He is like a double-agent." Edward redirects, "Anyhow, Holy will be on the lookout for the shrew." Lexa adds "If he finds him, will he engage in some serious 'Taming.... of the Shrew'. Get it? Taming of the Shrew. You know Shakespeare?" She laughs loudly. Harley looks at Lexa and rolls her eyes. Juni also looks at Lexa then shakes her head side to side. Both quickly refocus their attention on Edward. Lexa's laugh fades to quiet. Edward shoes the mole off on his mission. He quickly disappears down his hole. "Holy will report back once he gets some intelligence."

Edward motions us to follow him for the second phase of his plan. We follow him back to the dorms. Luciana is just waking up. She appears more relaxed. Edward directs, "Luciana, you and Andi will go back to the lab. Juni, Lexa and Harley, your mission is to gain possession of the ashes. Luciana and Andi will circle around and join your mission if they get theirs done in time. Our post will be the Learning Center at the pharm. We form a circle and put our hands on top of each other's like we're in a football huddle or The Musketeers.

"We are a team" says Edward. Lexa adds "Team Whitches." She spells it out and informs us that the word is a combination of white (magic) and witches merged together. "It's sort of like Bradgelina. Before they split." Lexa laughs.

We break the huddle and divide into mission teams. Luciana and I head toward SMT and the Biology Department lab. It's a warm summer's night. I take a deep breath. My steps are resolute. Luciana seems to have lost her anxiety. It is amazing how betrayal and attempted murder can be offset by a good nap. On the way, I think about the words that came into my head during my last meditation. "Black rock." Suddenly it hits me like a ton of bricks. Slate or Dr. Slater. Slate is a black rock. Hopefully I will become more adept at understanding these premonitions. Just as I think this, I hear the High Priestess' voice in my head "Soon you won't have to meditate. This information will just pop into your head." I thank Gertrude. She replies, "Success on your mission. Bring me home." Luciana looks at me in my distracted state. She says "focus" in a bossy manner.

We get to SMT. I try the door but it is locked. I look around to find another way into the building. I concentrate. Luciana steps in front of me, smiles, reaches into her pocket and produces a key. She proceeds to unlock the door. "That will work." We head to the basement. The lights are out and there is no sign of anyone in the lab. Luciana head toward the UPLC and I head toward the sample storage room to try the combination we used before, 15-32-7. The drawer opens but it's empty. I thought it was worth a try.

Luciana is running a sample in the dark. She points to a work bench. It has a powdery substance on it. I assume it's the remnants of the High Priestess' ashes. Luciana appears to be running a test from Dr. Slater's messy sample preparation. I sweep the rest of the powdery substance into a small sample baggie. I place it carefully and respectfully into my pocket. I check to make sure it is deep in my pocket, so it won't fall out accidentally.

The instrument's computer prints out several pages of data. Luciana types in additional commands and an addition printout comes out that infers an expanded 3-D pattern of the DNA structure. Luciana tears off the results and puts them in her pocket. She enters more commands and the computer responds. Luciana highlights the name of the program then hits the delete button. Eric's saved results from his earlier test of the High Priestess' ashes disappear. She turns around to leave but changes her mind and returns to the terminal.

She speaks aloud as she goes back into Eric's files. "This is Eric's rough draft of his research publication for tenure. D-e-l-e-t-e-d!" She smiles with satisfaction. She shuts down the instrument. "Let's go." I start to follow her but see my favorite overshirt on a chair. I grab it as we go out the door. I need this shirt to hide Sam in, now that I can fully trust her again.

We run across campus. The sun is getting low in the sky. There are white billowy clouds coming in from over the bay. I'm out of breath as we reach the Learning Center. The mole is there and eating insects that have been hand-picked from the crops on the pharm. Edward smiles, feeling proud that he can use organic methods to get rid of the pests on his crops and reward Holy at the same time. Lexa, Juni and Harley are preparing to go on their mission. Lexa has blackened her face with what looks like a large amount of mascara. She is helping the others to camouflage themselves during nighttime. She starts rubbing black mascara on Juni's face. Juni looks at her like she is crazy and slaps her hand. "I am already naturally camouflaged."

Lexa puts down the mascara. She looks down at the mole and his plate of food. "That is guaca-mole'. When he bends down over his dish like that, he shows us his mole-asses." Lexa snorts a little as she laughs to herself. Lexa quickly grabs her abdomen and grunts. I turn to Luciana. "She makes jokes when she is nervous. She also gets intestinal distress." Luciana gives a look to say, TMI for Too Much Information. Lexa burps loudly. Luciana adds "You are mole-esting the mole." Of course, she is referring to the word molestar meaning "to bother" in Spanish.

Harley and Juni head out toward campus, leaving Lexa behind. Lexa runs to catch up with them. She limps as she runs. I yell out to her to watch for "mole holes." Luciana and I wait for a few minutes before we follow the other three. They briskly walk toward main campus, off the brick path, using the shelter of the building to conceal their presence. We continue to follow a building behind them.

I survey the area. There is movement near the trees to the right of the building. I look to see a beautiful full tail of a fox. It is nice to know Emelie is thinking of us. I look the other way and see a small, black creature coming across the grass. As it gets closer, I recognize her. I wonder how Sam got out of the dorm room. I look north and see a blacktail deer on the steps between the department buildings. I comment to Luciana "Everyone seems to be in place." We continue to follow Juni, Harley and Lexa across campus. I notice they stop abruptly at Red Square. I look to see why they stopped. I point at the telltale hot head characteristic of smoking drugs in a glass pipe. The Darksiders are having a gathering at the Skyview sculpture. Juni leads Harley and Lexa in retreat then crosses over to the west side of campus so they will not be detected. I'm grateful that the Darksiders are too oblivious or intoxicated to notice us.

Luciana and I join Juni, Harley and Lexa at the business college. We stand out of the range of the light from an overhead lamp. We split up and check all entryways to find a possible point of entry. Everything is locked. I appreciate Shamita's close attention to security, although it is not helpful to our mission.

I can hear yelling and loud talking coming from the sculpture. The Darksiders seem to like to party. However, their IQ seems to drop as the party goes on. I check my watch. We have plenty of time before our powers wane and their powers amplify.

I look up as I hear a buzzing overhead. The buzzing moves quickly from place to place, then into the light of an overhead lamp. For a brief moment, I see a hummingbird stop and hover in the light. Harley smiles and waves to her friend before the bird disappears. The humming sound fades. Harley tries a window next to her. It opens even though she thought she previously checked it and it was locked. She crawls through the small opening and vanishes into the darkness of the building. We wait in silence for some time. Lexa starts to get anxious. She rubs her abdomen to calm it. Then there is a clicking noise. The main door opens with Harley on the other side. We take the elevator up to the ninth floor then take a right to office number 999. I shake my head at how stereotypical the Darksiders are. 999 is 666 upside-down. There is a name plate on the door, "Dr. Swhart." Lexa grabs the doorknob and tries to turns it. It does not turn. The group let's out a discouraging sigh. Lexa smiles, indicating she was just joking. She then turns the doorknob. The office door was left unlocked. She pushes it open. Each of us gives Lexa a dirty look as we walk past her and into the office. We hear the sound of the hummingbird again but this time in the hallway. Harley looks proud as she exclaims, "That's how that window got unlocked."

Sid's office is nicely decorated with dark, antique wood and leather furniture. There is a dark Persian rug covering the floor and a large window with a wide-angle view overlooking Red Square. I walk over, pull up the blind and look out the window. There is a direct view of the Skyview sculpture. I automatically crouch down and move away from the window. I can see the Darksiders moving inside the sculpture.

We search the office for the ashes but can't find them. "Are you sure the mole said the ashes were here?" "Yes" Harley responds. "Edward said this is where the mole said they were." I pull out the drawers of the desk and flip them upside down. I look behind the paintings on the walls, feel the carpet and the inside the furniture. I rack my brain trying to think like a Darksider. I go over in my mind every possible hiding place. Thankfully the Police Department gave me experience in searching premises. I look down as I am thinking. My eyes are drawn to a plastic bag in the garbage can. I feel sick. I bend over and slowly pick up the plastic bag from the can. I cannot believe what I see. This is how Sid treats the ashes of his mother? I think I may vomit. I want to protect Emelie from this knowledge. I put the ashes in my pack.

Suddenly a light goes on down the hall. The light from the crevice under the office door lights up the floor of the room. I see the others looking for places to hide but there is nowhere to hide. Quickly Juni pulls out a long rope from her backpack. She ties it to one of the legs of the desk. She pushes the desk toward the window to give it leverage then throws the rope out the window. In a panic, Lexa pushes Juni out of the way and grabs onto the rope. Lexa quickly jumps out the window. I run over to the office door and lock it from inside. The others stand motionless, holding their breath. Luciana appears as if she may faint. I hear footsteps coming toward the office. I jump behind the door. I think back to the days of being a police officer and feel naked without my gun. I hear a key go into the lock and jiggle around, engage and the door knob starts to turn. I crouch, readying myself to defend or attack. I'm not sure which at this time. Down the hall, I hear an unusual sound and quick but light footsteps. "Oink, oink, oink." The oinking comes closer. The door opens slightly then arrests. I hear heavy footsteps running toward the oinking. Someone yells to another, "There's a pig in here! Get it." The voice and footsteps go down the stairwell and eventually they are heard outside.

I run to the window and look down. Lexa isn't below. I turn and see Lexa crouching on the ledge outside the window holding the rope in her hands. She is rigid and staring at the ground. "Lexa, are you alright?" Lexa is too scared to answer. I grab her and pull her back into the office. She is stiff with fear. "I feel sick." She is holding her gut. "I can't hold it." Lexa looks around then whips down her pants and sits on the garbage can that was next to Dr. Swhart's desk. She groans in pain and relief then reaches over the desk and picks up a monogrammed note pad. She uses this as toilet paper. Luciana covers her mouth trying to suppress a gag. I start to laugh. Lexa tells me to "go to hell." I reply, "I am already there from the smell." "Hurry up they may come back. You can thank Susy. She is our savior." We tidy up the office and leave the door slightly open. To air out the sewage stench coming from inside the office.

We exit the building. Lexa screams with anxiety as we go down the exterior stairs of the business department. "I almost died. What was I thinking to try and take a rope nine floors down to the ground?" "Yeah" Juni says. "The rope is only 50 feet long." "Next time we need to think through Plan B better." I add, "At least we have the ashes. This is most important."

As we come around the corner outside the building, there is someone in the shadows, leaning against the wall. I startle then focus on the figure. "Ladies, I heard a farm animal got loose from the farm. Apparently, it was a pig. Did any of you see a pig?" I recognize the voice. "Officer Tandori, I am so glad you are keeping order on campus and responding to urgent calls for missing pharm animals. It is vital that we get the pig back to its rightful place. To answer your question, we know nothing about a pig or any other run-away animal. If we see anything, we will assist the truant animal back to the Biodynamic Pharm for its safety and the safety of others." "Thank you" says Shamita. "This is not a zoo you know." "Yes, Officer Tandori. I will let Edward know. He probably forgot to close the gate." Shamita winks. "The sow surprised a couple of Dr. Swhart's teaching assistants. I guess they were trying to drop off graded term papers last minute." "Yes, I remember late nights as a student. Good night. I hope this incident didn't interrupt your donut break." Shamita laughs and salutes a good-bye.

"Let's get back. Emelie will be waiting" We stop back at the dorms to pick up our robes. Lawren was not there. She has been gone all day. Sam wasn't there either. We gather our belongings and head toward the pharm.

Chapter 15

The Anointing and Spreading of Ashes

It was dark and I could see a fire burning bright in the night at the pharm. Edward and Emelie are sitting around the fire drinking tea. Edward looks up and smiles. He pours steaming tea into five mugs that were waiting by the fire. "I just harvested some Holy Basil. Tulsi is a ceremonial tea. Tonight, is a special occasion for all of us and Andi. She will be anointed and we can finally lay to rest our former High Priestess." Emelie and Edward are dressed for the ceremony. Both are wearing a natural fiber blouse and slacks with ornate embroidery designs and colors. I packed my ceremonial robe to put on once I get to The Tree of Life. Luciana headed back to the dorms to wait for Lawren to return.

Susy and Sam are sitting near the fire waiting for us. The goat wanders over and sits next to them. At the perimeter of the glow from the fire I can see the fox and the deer. Lexa runs up to Susy and pats her forehead. She thanks her for saving us at Sid's office. Sam looks at me with her big, yellow eyes and rubs up against my leg. I grab her and give her a big hug. We hear the buzzing of a hummingbird's wings in the distance.

We light our candles and start our trek up Conundrum Hill in silence. I become mindful of the smells in the air, the sensation of my feet coming in contact with the earth, the sounds of the crickets and a soft breeze on my face. I tell my mind and body to relax with every step. The rhythm of my steps helps quiet my mind. I have become much more aware of my surroundings. I sense nocturnal animals in the distance, the life of the trees, the others on the trail and the energy in the moonbeams hitting my body. The world around me feels energetic and crawling with life. My senses are acute. I am pleased by these sensations.

It seems like we just started up the hill but when I look up, we are already at The Tree of Life. The tree's branches are majestic and highlighted by moon and sky in the background. There is a subtle trickling of the stream that feeds the pond next to the tree. The air is buzzing with excitement and anticipation.

I reach into my pack and pull out Sam. She is limp with sleep. I place her on a blanket then take out my robe. I carefully put it on and button it. It's not ornate as are Emelie's or Edwards robes. I line up the candles.

I carefully place a candle to represent each corner of the earth, north, south, east and west. Then I place smaller white candles in between these candles, more go around the pond, on the lower branches of the tree and on the jagged rocks erupting out of the sand. Someone even brought floating candles that are lit and set adrift on the pond. The light from the candles are so bright, it is easy to believe it is the middle of the day. I gaze at the different candles with their colored flames, flickering in unity. I smell the essential oils in the wax being released as the wax melts.

I sit on my knees in the middle of my blanket. The others surround me and Emelie sits facing me. She starts talking in another language. It is not a language I have heard before but it is familiar. She places her hands on my sacrum then follows my backbone upward. She stops in certain areas, says a foreign word or two then works her way up my back. She moves her hands around to the front of my body, pausing at my navel, my heart, my throat, my lower forehead then the crown of my head. She opens her arms and salutes the heavens. Emelie talks and sometimes sings as she does this. She brings her hands down and circles my upper body. She grabs a chalice of water, blesses it then sprinkles water onto my forehead. The water drips down my face. She continues to speak quietly in a foreign language. Emile raises a small decanter, pours oil into her palms then rubs her palms together. There is a faint perfume smell. She places her index finger into the palm of her hand then presses her oiled fingertip between my eyebrows. She anoints me with warm, sweet smelling oil. I feel the energy rising up my spine and between my eyebrows. The oil feels like it is on fire. I become dizzy and close my eyes so I don't fall over or vomit from dizziness. As I close my eyes, I see large amounts of information pass behind my eyelids. It feels like a strong wind is trying to blow me down. I automatically take a deep breath and think to myself how obvious this information is. It is all so simple. Why didn't I know this before? My head feels so heavy that I lose my balance and fall backwards. Emelie catches me and cradles my head. She directs the others to place their hands on me. I can feel each hand burn my skin as energy is transferred between us. I have an insight that we are all one. I see faces flash in front of my eyes. I know these people are my ancestors. The last people I see are Lady Madsen, Edward and Emelie. I become so tired. I can't move. I lay in an awkward position and drift off. I dream about the people behind the faces. In my dream, they know me and I feel loved by them.

I wake rejuvenated several minutes later. Harley, Lexa, Juni, Emelie and Edward are looking at me, waiting for me to wake. There are others from the coven who recently showed up. They are dressed in their robes and veils. They stand holding hands encircling us, the tree and the pond.

I feel warm and comfortable. Edward is tending a blazing campfire. I look down and see that I've been covered with a blanket. It appears to be handmade and intricately embroidered with different colors of thread. There are various designs but the main design takes up the majority of the blanket. It is a beautiful reproduction of The Tree of Life. Such handicraft must have taken years to stitch.

I look at Emelie. "I had a dream and, in my dream, I saw my ancestors. Lady Madsen, Edward and you were also there." Emelie smiles and cups my face. Edward stands behind me and places his hand on my shoulder. "Yes, my dear. You are our niece. I prayed this day would come. I needed to stay away from you. I didn't want to draw attention to you. The former High Priestess is your grandmother." I stutter, "You are my mother's sister? And Edward is my uncle? Lady Madsen is my grandma?"

"I also saw my mother in my dream. I haven't seen her for so long, I forgot what she looked like. I can see the resemblance in both of you. To live most of my life missing my family and now I have the two of you. My sisters were there also, even the one who died in a car accident."

"The blanket is yours. It is traditional for multi-generations to work on a blanket for their descendants. Your great-grandmother, grandmother, mother, your aunt and uncle worked on this blanket.

One generation starts the blanket then the next generation adds to it and so on." I hold the blanket close to my face. Tears well up in my eyes. I start sobbing in joy and grief. The joy is related to finding my new family and my grief is related to missing my old family, those that have passed.

"You are special. You are able to read The Stone Tablet. Most people can pick up The Tablet without anything happening. They must translate The Book of Knowledge and read it like a book. You were able to download this information instantly. You are obviously of the bloodline. Others in our family may also have this gift. One's calling, calls. It is up to you whether you answer and rise to the occasion. Although, natural talent and abilities are a small part of the equation. Most of it is a matter of choice. How do you choose to express yourself in this world? What legacy do you want to leave? How do you want to be remembered by your family, friends and acquaintances? Do you want to leave an impression? Is it a positive impression? Will you be viewed as an honorable and fair person? Will you contribute to the world in some sort of way? These are questions you must answer. We are beings of free will. With free will comes responsibility. We can choose good or bad. You can join the Whitches or the Darksiders. It is up to you. Enough lecturing for now, my dear. Now it is time to bury your grandmother."

I take out the ashes of former High Priestess, Gertrude Madsen, from my backpack. Now I know why her portrait in the library seemed familiar. I met her when I was a small child. To think I am now holding her, that is, what's left of her, in my hands. I wish I had the opportunity to get to know her. I give Emelie the plastic bag of ashes.

Emelie addresses the four corners, north, south, east and west. She looks to the sky and says a prayer, thanking the universe for High Priestess Madsen. She acknowledges the miracle of her birth, life and the completion of her life cycle to death. Emelie places the ashes, in different quantities into four chalices. She adds water to one of the chalices. She speaks, "You will return to the four elements and The Tree of Life. You are to return to where you came. You have completed one cycle of the circle. The circle has no beginning and no end. I shall return you to the earth, so you can continue the circle of life. The many circles of life. Birth, life, death. Death, life, birth, and so on." Emelie takes the chalice and dips it in the stream above the pond. She allows the ashes to flow out of the chalice and down the stream. She blesses the ashes that are floating, and the heavier ashes that have sunk, and asks them to find their way to the next incarnation of Lady Madsen. Sail with the element of Water.

Emelie picks up another chalice and ceremoniously walks around The Tree of Life. Edward uses a large stick to make a small trench around the tree. Emelie follows him and pours the dry ashes into the trench. She gives another blessing. "You return to The Tree of Life through the Earth. You return to the family tree, back to those you belong to and to who you belong." Edward circles around again to close the trench with the stick, burying the ashes, mixing them with the Earth. Emelie takes another chalice.

Emelie walks past the pond and toward the edge of the hill. "The element of Air sets you free. It symbolizes the detachment from the body. You are now free to drift in the wind. Air is the element that gives life and breath." Emelie throws the ashes over the hill and down the cliff. "May the breeze bring you back to us." Emelie rubs her hands together. She walks over and picks up the last chalice. "Last but not least, Fire is an element that can symbolize anger and destruction. This is an element not commonly used by the whitches but Lady Madsen was able to command this force. May the Fire symbolize your transition of being from one form to another. Fire causes the spirit to break away from the bone and rise to the heavens, leaving the physical behind and becoming spirit. May your spirit be free from the physical pain associated with being on this plane." Emelie tosses the ashes into the fire. As the ashes meet the flames, they spark and turn into white smoke. The smoke ascends upward rising toward the heavens. "So, it is. As is in heaven, so on earth."

Emelie turns toward us. I can see a tear fall down her cheek. "She was a good whitch and I miss her. Let's continue to celebrate her life with food and drink." We sit on the blanket, near the fire and the pond. Edward breaks out some pear wine. He fills each of our chalices. We raise our chalice for a toast. As our chalices touch, making a clinking noise, a falling star catches my eye. It bursts into flames. Emelie says, "That is mom winking at us." We toast the remnants of the falling star. More witches from our coven have come from the forest on all sides. They hold hands making a large circle around us, the pond and The Tree of Life. They quietly hum. I can feel their support. Some are crying in grief, feeling the loss of the former High Priestess.

I kneel down for an addition to the tattoo that was already

started on the back of my neck. Carefully a trunk of the tree is added to the preexisting root system. My anointment and my ability to access The Stone Tablet advances me to a Level 2 whitch before the others. The ceremony makes my advancement official. It is witnessed by the entire coven. I look across the crowd and see Officer Tandori. She walks toward me, gives me a hug and whispers in my ear "Sorry I can't acknowledge you in my ceremonial wear because I'm still on the clock." She holds the embrace for an extended period of time before allowing others to congratulate me from the long line that has formed behind her.

Chapter 16

An Urgent Call for Betrayal: WWW

After pear wine, song and dance, the four of us stumble back to the dorms. It is approximately 11:30. Luciana is in the dorm room. She is relieved we are back. She is afraid to be alone since the incident earlier this afternoon. Lawren has not returned to the dorms and I'm nervous about her safety. My head is foggy from the wine and my balance is slightly off. Edward makes a powerful pear wine that hits with a powerful punch. I know I'm not in great condition but I have a feeling that the Darksiders have Lawren. A voice tells me to go to the northwest side of campus where the Performing Arts Auditorium is located.

The Performing Arts Auditorium or referred to as PAA but sounds like PAW, is located at the northwest edge of campus. It butts up to a large, brick plaza that overlooks the bay. In the center of the plaza is a substantial, orange, triangular sculpture named "For Handel". It is made from heavy-duty construction steel that looms into the sky. I used to hang out there during lunchtime as a student. I would buy cheap pizza from Pizza Plaza that was located just off the brick plaza. I would either sit on the plaza or stand behind the raised flowerbeds. The flowerbeds act as a barrier to protect students from falling several stories down to the street below. The height gives a wonderful view of the bay.

I tell the others "Lawren may need us." They stop what they are doing and look at me. "Come on." The five of us dash out of the dorms and head across the dark campus. As I rush toward the PAA, information goes through my head. It's obvious I no longer need to meditate to have access to information. I visualize the sculpture's triangular shape and automatically receive information on The Power of a Triangle. "The triangle symbolizes many things in many cultures and religions. In Christianity is symbolizes the Trinity. In other cultures, it symbolizes principles such as Gender, Ascension and Manifestation or Past, Present and Future or Creation, Preservation and Destruction or Creator, Sustainer and Destroyer or Birth, Life and Death." The latter symbolism makes me anxious. I can feel the breeze from the west coming off the bay. The triangular sculpture comes into view as there are accent lights to illuminate the sculpture in the dark. The campus is quiet except the dozen or so people at the sculpture. I can see Lawren. She is smiling and laughing with Odious and Nefara. She appears to be smoking a marijuana cigarette. I put my arms out stopping the others in their tracks. We stand staring, trying to figure out what to do. Another burst of cool air hits me in the face. I wonder, "Is Lawren one of the Darksiders?" I'm not sure if I should be protecting Lawren from the Darksiders or protecting us from Lawren.

I see Sid sitting on the sculpture above the others. Below is Odious, Nefara and Lawren standing very close to each other. Odious leans over to kiss Lawren on the cheek. Lawren appears to welcome his affection. Nefara leans in, nudging Odious out of the way and kisses Lawren on the mouth. Nefara presses her body into Lawren's. Lawren responds by passionately engaging in the kiss. Lexa exclaims "I feel like I am watching a slutty episode of the L-Word." I comment, "It's more like Catherine Deneuve in The Hunger." Juni declares, "And I thought I was special. It appears they like Lawren even more than they liked me this afternoon." There is a hint of jealousy in her tone.

We crouch down by the steps that lead from the central street of the campus to the brick plaza. We watch the dark interaction in disbelief. Lawren doesn't look as if she has been captured or coerced. I feel a blanket of sickness with a hint of betrayal, slither down my throat and into the abyss of my stomach. I look at my watch. "It is close to midnight. I think our work is done here." The wave of nausea continues to flow over me, pushing me slightly off balance. I look to the horizon to steady myself but I can barely see the separation between the sky and bay as the night grows darker. "Come on ladies. We don't want to turn into bitter, green whitches" says Lexa. We slowly walk back to the dorms.

Chapter 17

The Rule of Three-Fold

I wake up to knocking at the shared bathroom door. I locked it last night after we returned from the PAA. I pick up Sam who is curled up on my stomach. She appears annoyed by the disturbance. I look over at Harley as I go to answer the door. Harley encourages me to open the door with a wave of her hand. I pull down my top and pull up my bottoms of my pajamas which have rolled up and down in either direction while I was sleeping. I slowly open the door with apprehension. Of course, it's Lawren. She is wearing the same clothes she was wearing two days ago. Her hair is disheveled and her pants have creases that are made from sleeping in one's clothes.

I ask "What time is it?" Lawren is pale. "I don't know" Lawren sighs. I look at my cell phone "It's six o'clock." She tries to run her fingers through her hair but they get caught in a tangled ball of hair. She gives up and pulls her fingers out. She has a large indistinguishable stain on her shirt. "Yes, Lawren?" I notice my manner is cold. She grumbles, "Do you have any crackers to settle my stomach?" I just stand staring at her. Harley jumps out of bed and hands Lawren some whole grain crackers. Lawren slowly brings a cracker to her mouth. She chews slowly, holding back the urge to vomit. Her mouth appears dry and dry bits of cracker fly out as she speaks. "I can't believe the last two days. I feel sick. I was raised to be a good Jewish girl. I studied hard, earned my Ph.D. and always did the responsible thing." I try to look like I am concerned and empathetic but I could barely look at her. "Well, you guys left me at the dorms. You took off without saying a word. I was upset, so I went across campus. There was a group of people I recognized from one of the events we attended. They were friendly, especially Odious and Nefara. Anyhow, they asked me to join them. They took me to dinner, a movie in the downtown district, then we went to a hotel and had drinks. We ended up at Dr. Swhart's house. He has a really nice home overlooking the bay. There were others, it was like a two-day party. Anyway, they all treated me so well. Just like I was family. I told them I had a neck ache, so they hired a masseuse to come to the house to give me a massage. I was really tired after that and ended up falling asleep in the spare bedroom. When I woke up everyone was still there. They took me out for breakfast at a nice restaurant in Safehaven district. Things just continued until early this morning. I feel so awful. They had drugs and I don't even use drugs. They also had alcohol. I rarely drink but I drank and smoked marijuana. My behavior was so out of character. I guess I felt safe with them. They were so caring and nice. They took care of me and catered to my every need. Even needs I didn't know I had. I could not say no to them. I've never been so impressionable or reckless in my life. I don't know what came over me. I felt as if I could trust them inherently. I even made out with a couple of them, at the same time, which again is totally out of my character. It was as if I was under a spell and no longer making my own decisions."

"Then a really weird thing happened early this morning. I looked out the window and saw a deer. It was just standing there. I remember it having a black tail. It was as if the deer was looking right at me and only me. I looked back into her soft brown eyes. She turned away and I felt compelled to follow her. I was able to walk up to her, almost touching her, then she would take a couple steps and wait for me to catch up again. Once I got away for Sid and his gang, it's as if my judgment returned. I became sick and vomited in the middle of Red Square due to disgust for my own behavior. Anyway, the deer lead me back to the dorms. As soon as I got to my dorm, the doe disappeared into the forest behind the Biodynamic Farm. I need a bath with some disinfectant to wash away the last couple days. Please don't let me do that again. I feel like I just dodged a cult. Can I lay down on your bed?" Harley and I direct Lawren to my bed. The blankets are still warm from my body. Lawren puts down the last part of a cracker she was trying to eat. She quickly curls up and closes her eyes. I can smell vomit in her hair and a body odor that accumulates without a regular shower. She mumbles as she drifts off to sleep. "Sid keeps talking about his plan to cut down an old tree tonight." Lawren falls into a deep sleep.

The others run to catch up with me as I run toward the Biodynamic Pharm. "Andi, wait." I continue with determination. There is no one at the pharm, so I continue to the forest until I reach the large, old growth tree. I pull down the ladder and climb up. There is a fire burning in the living room where Emelie and Edward are sitting. Edward is in an old rocking chair made from tree branches. Emelie is sitting across from him on a small couch. They are both leaning over a small table and appear to be playing a game. I call out to Emelie. "They are going to cut down The Tree of Life." Emelie does not look up. She continues to roll what looks like dice. Some of the faces of the die are blank while others have symbols on them. She rolls eight dice. The dice appear to be made out of fossilized wood. They look ancient. Emelie and Edward lean over the table. "Look Edward." She pushes the dice into groups and studies each group.

Emelie looks concerned then raises her arms toward the sky. Suddenly there is a downpour of rain and a flash of lightning with no thunder after it. The rain feels electric. A warm wind blows through the window of the tree-house. "How dare they. This is our sacred place. Until now both sides have respected each other's sacred place." In the distance, I hear dogs howling, then cows, donkeys, goats, chickens as they join, in concert. Animals from the forest and the hill unite in the mix. There is commotion outside. I hear bushes being disturbed and the sound of feet and hooves in motion on the ground. The rain, wind and lightning continue.

"This is our warning signal. It notifies other whitches of an imminent concern and sends a warning to the Darksiders. They know we are coming. You can compare it to an air raid siren warning system. This is a World War of the Witches. The dice foretell this. See this group of dice? Here is The Skull and the Dark Witch. Over there is The Tree, The Dark Side of the Moon and see these symbols? Emelie points in another direction, and this group has The Tablet and The Chalice.

Edward jumps up, then goes down on all fours to the floor. He pulls up a floor board then takes out an old skeleton key from below. He walks over to the trunk of the tree that is in the center of his living room. He pulls back a façade of bark and inserts the key into an old iron lock. A compartment opens. Edward reaches inside and takes out a weathered book. Edward speaks softly, "This is our emergency book. It contains information that is to be used only in an emergency. This is only half of the information needed. The other half of the book is located at the Ancient Library. We don't store the two parts of the book together. This way no one can get access to the complete information at once. It protects us in case there is a breech in our system by an outsider, or a Darksider and protects us from using this powerful magic on impulse."

"Luciana go stay with Lawren. It is unsafe for either of you to be alone. The rest of us will meet at the library. This is my emergency exit, it will get you there faster." He pushes her through a pair of open French doors, onto a small balcony and sits her in a waiting swing seat attached to a zipline. She lets out a long cry that wavers as she speeds down the line. I lose sight of her as she disappears through the trees headed toward Safehaven dorms.

Emelie and Edward grab our hands. They chant, pull us down the ladder to the ground then face us toward the library. Stationary objects blur in front of my eyes and I feel the movement of air on my face. We are walking but the objects around us seem to be moving faster than we are. I focus ahead and see that we are already at the library. Edward puts in the code and we are at the shelves of books. He picks up a book, peels away the outside of the book revealing a smaller book inside. He thumbs through the pages written in the Witches Alphabet. I can see some of the words but not enough to understand what they are saying. He makes symbols in the air with the finger of his left hand. I feel my body lift and float. The others are floating also. We are still holding hands. Emelie draws symbols in the air also, which pulls us toward the purple stained glass. The room is a bright purple with bits of suspended light drifting in the air. I can sense the Darksiders are on the other side of the stained glass. We continue to float upward, toward and through the stained glass. It is as if our bodies have become particles of light and lose their solid form. On the other side of the stained glass is the pond that is fed by the stream. As we go through the stained glass and through the water, I notice a change in the pressure. The water presses against my body. I hold my breath but realize I can breathe under water. The oxygen inside the water freely flows inside and out of my body, exchanging oxygen for carbon dioxide. My body feels refreshed and oxygenated. As we emerge through the water there is another change in pressure. The air pulls and lifts my body making me feel weightless like a balloon. Emelie makes another symbol and everything slows down. We have emerged from the pond totally dry. We land lightly onto the sandy ground between the pond and the tree.

I look around to see many others. I am trying to compute what is happening. I sense some are whitches and others are Darksiders. Sid, Odious and Nefara are standing at the trunk of The Tree of Life. Sid is projecting an intense energy bolt while Odious and Nefara are supporting him with their powers. He raises the bolt toward the trunk to cut it. The other Darksiders stand on the far side of the tree as our coven of whitches stand opposite in a face-off. The whitches simultaneously raise their hands getting ready to retaliate.

Emelie calls out to Sid to stop. "This is your ancestry as well as ours. Regardless whether you want to acknowledge it or not. This tree holds the remains of all of your ancestors. It is a symbol of our customs. It is where we come to worship. This is their resting place and our sacred place. We have agreed that our sacred places are off limits for retribution or revenge. Discontinue your actions and retreat. We will not say another word about this incident and will continue to honor our agreement." As she says this the blazing bolt becomes brighter and hotter. The other Darksiders have joined in by contributing their powers to the bolt.

Emelie raises her voice, "If you choose to continue, your actions will signify out and out war. We will retaliate and desecrate your sacred grounds as well. We prefer to coexist in peace. You have a right to your beliefs and religious practices as we have a right to ours. As long as you do not harm others." Sid responds, "You could ask mom what happened when she crossed me. That is, if she were still alive."

Emelie retorts, "Mother did not cross you, you crossed her. You never respected her values. She was heartbroken by your disregard for our customs and your interest in the dark powers. She could not understand why you picked the dark practices when you could have built up our coven and the community by emulating her. Instead you took all of your accumulated knowledge and power to work against everything she believed in."

Sid breaks in. "I found your present in the garbage can in my office. The same garbage can that I threw away mother's ashes. A fitting burial for an unfit mother. Don't you feel it a coincidence that mother died by a force that is primarily used by the Darksiders? I picked up the mastery of fire from mom. I DID emulate her and even surpassed her skill of fire. Uncontrolled, the element of fire consumed her, returning her to the elements of the earth. Such a waste of unfulfilled talent. I should have succeeded mother to lead the witches out of the dark ages of the craft. They would realize that I am the chosen one. Instead, they elected you, sister, to lead them. If she could see you now. How you turned out and how the coven has suffered under your leadership."

The air is charged. I can feel my hair standing on end. Both sides reeving up for the ultimate confrontation. The wind blows swiftly and dark clouds move in. Lightning strikes in a series of explosions. Birds flock together and fly in circles, high in the sky. I hear barks, howls, chirps and bellows from various species of animals. I look down at the campus to see the lights go out. The campus falls into blackout. The stream leading to the pond becomes heavier and wider. The pond fills and becomes rough with currents and waves.

Sid lowers the bolt of energy that he is holding above the tree trunk. It hits the bark of the trunk. I can smell the aroma of burnt bark in the air. I'm distracted by the sound of running water behind me. As I turn to look, I see the stream has widened and grown fuller and stronger. It is causing the pond to overflow its banks. High waves have developed in the center of the pond. They peak and separate. A tower of water rises in the middle of a trough that has formed. It reaches about ten feet in height. Colors swirl in the tower. Purple, blue, yellow then red. An image forms. An image that I have become more and more familiar with. It is the former High Priestess. I say to myself, "grandma?" She is a beautiful woman. I can feel her strength. I sense a feeling of respect coming from others in my coven and fear coming from the Darksiders. Lady Madsen's lips are pursed with anger.

"Sid, I knew you disrespected me. It's common for boys to resent and reject their mother at times. You never grew out of this phase. You internalized hatred for me, as well as for other women. I'm not sure what I did to fail you. I knew you were angry but never thought you were angry enough to commit murder. You destroyed the person who was responsible for your creation. Maybe this is your own self-hatred. It is at the very least ironic. Whatever the case, I never thought you had it in you to destroy everything that we are. This tree has been the symbol of our presence on Conundrum Hill for over four hundred years. Our ancestors grafted and nurtured this tree and when they died, they were buried here. Their remains have been assimilated into this tree. It represents the branches of our genealogy, our foundation and our destiny."

I look over at Sid. He initially appeared shocked and scared but as the High Priestess continued to speak, his face turned beet-red with anger. He pulls back from cutting into the tree trunk. He lifts the bolt and comes down on a large branch emerging out the side of the trunk. The branch falls away from the tree with ease and onto the ground. As the branch severs, an electrical discharge disperses into the air. The circle of whitches and Darksiders stand staring at the fallen branch and the aftershock it caused. Both sides understand this offense could have dire consequences.

Sid looks down at the severed branch with pride. He then looks up at the image of his mother with contention. He lifts the bolt of energy again and moves it in the direction of the trunk. He appears to be enjoying his dominion. The other Darksiders have withdrawn their power and stand watching in disbelief as Sid continues to escalate like a teenager showing off in front of his friends. The High Priestess looks to the sky, conjures the spirits of the Ones Who Have Gone Before. Gertrude chants "As you do onto others, so is done onto you, threefold."

Sid smirks as he touches the bolt to the trunk of the sacred tree. A warm stream of air flows down the hill and through the leaves of the tree. It makes ripples in the stream and pond as if flows over the top of the water. I see images of women and men in the water. As his bolt touches the bark, Sid yells out in pain. The High Priestess repeats "As you do onto others, so is done onto you, threefold." She continues, "From this day forward, as done onto The Tree of Life, so is done onto the you." Within the breeze, multiple low toned voices can be heard in the whitches language. I recognized these voices as the voices of my ancestors. They are repeating various protective spells. These sounds come from all directions in stereo.

I see that Sid's pant leg below his bolt of energy is torn and he is bleeding. He cries out in pain. The bolt of energy coming from his hands becomes dim then disappears completely. Elusive thunder cracks in the sky then an unyielding hail storm hits half of the circle of witches, only the Darksiders. The hail pelts them in the face, head and other exposed skin, causing red marks. They scatter like cockroaches once the lights have been turned on. Sid stands there alone, bleeding and whimpering in pain. He looks around becoming cognizant the he has been abandoned by his clan. He disappears in a dim flash of light under the dark sky. The hail ends and the warm air becomes cooler then stops flowing. High Priestess Gertrude's image becomes faint. She whispers "Goodbye my daughter, Aurora my son, Edward and granddaughter, Orenda. Take care of the coven. Our future depends on you." Her image sinks back down into the pond. The chanting from Those Who Have Gone Before stops. It is quiet.

The clouds dissipate. The stars shine bright in the morning sky. Building by building, the campus lights up, as the electricity comes back on. I notice my skin feels hot and sweaty against the cool air. Drops of sweat trickle down the center of my chest. The muscles in my legs feel shaky as if I just exercised to fatigue. I look at Emelie. She has a trail of tears running down her face. I hug and hold her. She wraps her arms around me and whispers, "I miss mom." At that moment, I feel the filling of an empty space that has been hollowed inside of my heart. I feel connected in a way I haven't felt for so long. Finally, I know the part of my family that I have been missing. Emelie holds my hand as we walk down the hill and back to the campus.

We gather around the campfire at the pharm. Edward serves a vegetable soup that he has been cooking since early this morning. I feel like I haven't eaten in a week. The broth is thick and salty. It sooths my throat and stomach with its warmth. Its sustenance calms my shaky muscles and vigilant nerves. I feel like a soldier who has just returned from battle. I'm happy to be with my family and friends in a safe circle around the fire. I rip off a piece of multi-grain bread from a sourdough loaf that was warmed over the campfire. I wash it down with pear cider that Edward pressed from The Tree of Life. The juice from these pears are very sacred.

Emelie raises her chalice for a toast, "To friends", we all take a sip. "To family. And so, it is." We take another sip. "To friends who become family. To all the friends and family who shape our lives." We take two sips. With each sip the cider becomes sweeter and more flavorful.

Edward announces that a little mole told him that Dr. Slater is working on a research project to find a substance that will extend life expectancy. He's aiming to stop aging all together so that the Darksiders can live forever. "Just think of it. If they live forever, they can amass experience, associates, alliances and networks to advance their self-interest. They can acquire wealth over centuries versus decades. They can continue to work on their personal goals until mastered. Their personal power will essentially continue to accumulate. They will no longer have to work against the clock to make achievements during their natural lifespan. They will be unstoppable."

Emelie adds another point of view. "Maybe Mother Nature gives us a finite length of time to live for a reason? Maybe our time here is meant to be short in contrast to the age of the universe. Maybe we are meant to do other things in other places, once we transition?"

Edward smiles as he continues with additional provocative information. "A little mole also told me that Dr. Slater is doing this to save his research grant with the Business Department. It seems that Dr. Slater failed to be successful with an epigenetic DNA project and this is a way to make amends, satisfy his grantors and save his neck." Luciana smiles at Edward in a knowing way.

Emelie looks concerned and announces "It's especially concerning if his research is only going to be available to certain people and not to the general population. This would only benefit the privileged." Lawren adds, "It seems to be a repeating pattern in history, doesn't it?" "Yes, Lawren it does. It is the same abuse of power and knowledge that has gone on throughout history. This is why it's our job to empower those around us rather than hold power to ourselves. This is why mentoring and passing down skills, history and tradition are so important. This is why new knowledge must be shared, so all can benefit and use this information as a stepping stone for advancement of the human race. We must give back and invest in others. This is the circle of life."

"A while back, I befriended someone. We met at the faculty Christmas party. I like to refer to it as the Solstice Party. Anyhow, her name is Dania, formally Dan. She transitioned from male to female just before she became a professor at Wasgard. She works at SMT. I wonder if Dania can keep an eye on what Dr. Slater is up to? Luciana, do you know her?" "Yes", Luciana replies. "She turns heads in the department. Most men become very threatened once they find out Dania has transitioned. Anyway, Dania named herself after her aunt whom she loved with all of her heart. She was the one person who really knew Dania and loved the quintessence of her spirit.

Her original name Dan is the male form of is aunt's name. She now honors her aunt's name through her new identity."

Emelie continues, "We have some time after what happened tonight. My brother and his clan will be licking their wounds for a while. I know my brother is evil but I can't stop worrying whether he is alright. I guess that's what makes me different from him. I am so angry at him for murdering mother and since throwing her ashes in the garbage, but I still remember him as a little boy. He was a good younger brother. I took care of him and he admired me. We were so close. I don't know what happened to him. It was insidious. He slowly grew away from me and the family. He was captivated by the lifestyles of the Wall Streeters and the One-Percenters. It was if he was intoxicated by them. I never thought he would become the man he is now. I admit, he is very charming and generous at first, until he gets you under his fold. Then you realize, it's all about him. He becomes controlling and abusive. By this time, it is too late. The poor victim is already taken by him and his lifestyle. Their self-esteem becomes only a fragment of what it used to be. I guess it is possible to love and hate someone at the same time. I think of how I feel betrayed but then think about my mother. How she must have felt. The last thing she saw was her son, her own flesh and blood, who she brought into this world, burn her alive. I can't bear to think of this." Emelie takes a long sip of her cider then swallows. She holds her cup up to make another toast. "To mom, the most honorable High Priestess, who lost her sovereignty tragically and ironically." Emelie draws symbols in the air with her finger then looks up at the sky.

I ask Edward, "What herbs did you throw during the confrontation at The Tree of Life?" Edward smiles, "It was a Reconciliation formula. The combination of herbs is used for reconciliation. I was hoping to avoid an all-out war. I threw the herbs and they caught the air flowing down the hill. I thought the flow would release the herbs over Sid and his groupies. I guess I missed. Magic if funny. Sometimes it works, sometimes the effects are delayed and sometimes it doesn't work at all. It all depends on other variables, such as magic cast by others, strength of intent, timing, synergy and so forth. The herbs were fresh, so I am surprised they didn't work. I guess I will have to go back to the drawing board and develop another recipe."

Emelie asks, "Are you girls going home tomorrow?" We look

around at each other and nod our heads for yes. "I suggest we have
to have a party in the Safehaven Lounge. How about some music,
dancing and drumming?" We look at each other and shake our heads
in unison. I comment, "After the stress of today, I think we could blow
of some steam." Emelie smiles, "It's settled. Let's rest and freshen
up then meet in the lounge later. We'll dance, celebrate and say
goodbye."

Lawrence Anderson

Chapter 18

Take, Apply and Put into Practice

We meet on the patio below Safehaven College. Emelie unlocks the French doors to the lounge. As usual, Edward brought food that has been harvested from the pharm. His goat saunters behind him then stops to wait outside on the patio. Susy, the pig and the deer are tagging behind. I have Sam inside my shirt. I hold her tight and breathe in the smell of her fur. She always smells as if she just came from the groomers. Her fur smells fresh and clean. She leans into me and purrs as I cuddle her. I stop and listen. I vaguely hear the howl of a fox in the distance. Susy trots up to the door and grunts. She seems unhappy to be separated from Lexa. Harley seems a little sad that her hummingbird hasn't made an appearance. As I look out onto the patio, I see the goat jump onto the three-foot cement wall that borders the patio and plaza. He looks down at the others and nays. I smile to see our animal family has gathered with us.

Edward also brought food for the animals. He goes out to the patio, gives each one a little treat and pats them as they eagerly eat. Edward is always thoughtful in this way. He seems happy with himself once he returns and sets out his spread of food and beverages for us. Emelie turns down the lights in the lounge. She pulls drums and other instruments out of a blue velvet bag with a gold tie string. Juni sits down at the piano. She touches the keys lightly to warm up, playing scales then transitions to a melody. She repeats a catchy ditty that leads into a song. We toast each other with cherry cider and move our bodies to the melody of the music.

Juni plays some R & B. We are dancing, laughing and enjoying our cider when the French doors off the patio swing wide open. I stare in amazement as Sid makes a grand entrance. He is followed by Odious and Nefara. I ready myself for battle. I expected retaliation but not quite so soon. I am momentarily frozen by the shock of their entrance and can only stare in surprise. I sense something is very different with the trio. Sid is uncharacteristically jolly. He dances and smiles as he limps toward us. He is wearing the same torn pants as earlier. There is blood trailing down his leg onto his shoe. His leg is red and swollen. His limp is more pronounced than before. This interferes with his swagger on the dance floor.

He claps his hands as he dances up to Emelie and gives her a big hug. He releases her after a long embrace then continues to dance around the drumming circle. Juni stops playing and just sits and stares. Odious walks over to the sound system and puts on a disco music track. He and Nefara join Sid as they dance wildly with themselves. I look at Emelie and the others in astonishment. They look back at me with a shocked expression. Suddenly it dawns on me that Edward's herbs must have worked after all.

Sid's hair becomes wilder as he dances furiously. His white bangs flips side to side. Odious and Nefara enact old disco moves on each other. Their movements are awkward and stiff. If I wasn't so shocked, I would laugh. This is a one-hundred and eighty degree turn from a couple of hours ago. The three are almost cute out there, by themselves, smiling, laughing and dancing with no restraint. Emelie walks over to the sound system and stops the music. I think of how fitting this is, as Safehaven College is known for their "Undisco" dances, named so, in contempt of disco music. I chuckle to myself at the blasphemy.

Emelie looks at Sid. He runs up to her like a little boy on the playground and raises his hands as if he wants to play Patty Cake. Emelie raises her hands to meet his, then grabs his hands and pulls them down to his side. Sid addresses Emelie in a schoolboy's voice. "Emelie, I was holding this, but as a gesture of reconciliation I want to give it to you." He holds out several sheets of paper that are strung together from a computer print-out. "Here's mom's DNA analysis from Dr. Slater. If Eric was able to read this data, we would've had everything we needed to put an end to the witches. But I'm giving this to you in good faith and as a gesture of concession." Luciana grabs the data out of Sid's hand. "Oh, and here. This is the remainder of mom's ashes from the lab. These shouldn't get into the wrong hands. These ashes are sacred and should be buried at The Tree of Life with the rest of our ancestors. She was a good mother. I miss her. It is tragic how she died." Sid looks into Emelie's eyes, "Come on sister. Let's dance." Emelie guides Sid back onto the dance floor with the other two. She pushes a button on the sound system and the disco music resumes. The three idiots start dancing again. The song playing is Disco Inferno by the group The Trammps, "Burn baby burn! Disco inferno! Burn baby burn! Burn that mama down." Such a fitting song for Sid.

Emelie turns to Edward. "How long will your herbs last?" Edward shrugs and speculates. "An hour? It depends on how fast the herbs are metabolized. Since their lifestyle is poor, they drink and use drugs, they are not as healthy as most who take care of themselves and abstains from substances. I would guess about two hours. More or less." Emelie directs Luciana and Lawren to occupy the Darksider's attention. She grabs my hand. "Andi, you and the rest of the girls come with me. I need to repossess an item. A family heirloom. We walk toward the edge of campus. Emelie walks slowly. She appears tired. I ask her if she is okay. She looks at me, "As whitches we don't have infinite strength or powers. Earlier I expended a large amount of energy. Thankfully I had help from the Former High Priestess, you girls and the rest of the coven, but I feel very tired. We have had several busy and trying days. I wish I could speed up time and get to our destination sooner but I don't have the strength. Therefore, I must pick and choose how I use what energy I have left."

We reach the west edge of campus then cut through the Safehaven District. Safehaven District is a district in Baypoint that is on the southwest side of the city. The district is known for its 19th century style architecture. Its history dates back to the late 1800's during the time of the railroads. Safehaven was competing to be a major terminal for The Great Northern Railroad. In those years, Safehaven District was actually its own town. In the early 1900's, it consolidated with three other cities, to become Baypoint. The word Safe Haven is the translation from the Native American term for "safe port" or "quiet place." The original name was "see-see-lich-em."

I learned this in one of our Core Classes during my first year at Safehaven College. Safehaven's history is mandatory for all new students. Each member of the faculty taught a segment of this class. Emelie taught the history of Conundrum which is the district where Conundrum Hill is located. This explains why she knows so much about the hill.

We walk past the apartments where I used to live as a student. It was the type of apartment that has a private bedroom and bathroom with a communal kitchen. Those were the days when I didn't have much money. It wasn't so bad living as a minimalist. We pass the old church that was converted into a residential housing rental. Once, I was invited to a Rugby party there. I didn't know the person who invited me. It was an acquaintance of a friend. Anyhow, when I got there, I was shocked to see the party was held in the former sanctuary area. A hot tub was conveniently placed where the pulpit used to be. There were dozens of student athletes in the hot tub at various levels of intoxication and undress. Even in those days of exploration that is characteristic of the college years, this seemed very sacrilegious.

We head down a hill toward the Baypoint Bay. I taste a salty breeze as we draw closer to the bay. We cross a main street of Safehaven District then cut down toward the bay via a residential neighborhood. We hit South Baypoint Trail that goes from Safehaven District, north to downtown Baypoint. It's a nice evening for a walk but I was wondering where we were going and concerned whether we would have enough time before Sid and his entourage converted back to themselves. Emelie suddenly turns off the trail, traverses through the shrubs and down to the water. Edward follows behind her without question, as if he knew where she was going. I hesitate then continue to follow behind them. The decline is steep and I start sliding on the top of small rocks and dirt, down the hill. Thankfully, I was able to slow down my momentum by grabbing onto the branches of small trees and shrubs. I motion for the others behind me to watch their step but it was too late for Harley. She slides into the back of me then falls on her bottom. Juni slowly weaves her way down the hill to decrease the effects its topography. Lexa comes down using a controlled slide like a skier.

Emelie and Edward continued downward over some large boulders that border the water's edge. Emelie reaches the bay and keeps walking, right into the water without even rolling up her pant legs. The water rises above her ankles and to her knees. Her pants wick up the water making a water mark halfway up her thigh. She stops, looks up at the sky, raises her arms with her palms upward, then closes her eyes and becomes quiet. We all follow her, getting into the water, stopping just as the water gets to our knees, like baby ducklings following their mother for a swim. I see that Emelie is connecting to the energy freely provided by the universe. Quickly the color returns to her face and her body stands strong as it breaks the ripples of saltwater drifting toward the shore. We grab each other's hands, make a circle facing outward and close our eyes. Immediately, I can feel the energy come up through the soles of my feet, climb my spine and continue up to the crown of my head. A wave of energy flows through my hand to Harley's hand then continues in a circuit around the circle. I experience an awareness and sensitivity to all the living things around me. Even the water in the bay feels alive. The waves of energy rejuvenate my body. This sensation is followed by a sense of unconditional love and wellbeing. Once renewed, we opened our eyes and released our hands, breaking the circle.

Emelie turns to lead us out of the water, up the shore and back onto the trail. We continue heading north toward downtown. Emelie's pace has quickened and her steps more determined. She finally speaks. "Sid has something that belongs to the family of whitches. Like your amber necklace, Sid also has a necklace. I didn't understand the significance of his when it was given to him but now, I do. Animal totems have specific traits related to the nature of the animal. These can be positive or negative attributes. It depends on how a person develops themselves whether these traits are good or bad. Sid's amber contains the fur of a Coyote. The coyote represents the "bringer of the seeds of life, bringing new life, new ways, using his instincts, cleverness and resourcefulness to serve the pack. He can use these gifts to transform the pack. The flip side of these qualities is being a shapeshifter, trickster, rebellious, fearless, and cocky or having reckless high energy. Does this sound familiar? The amber holds the energy of the animal it came from and this energy is compounded by the energy of the prayer and rituals performed on this totem. I want to take this opportunity to repossess this precious heirloom. The Darksider's sacred place is an abandoned industrial plant on the northern tip of Baypoint Bay, at the end of this trail. The plant was built in the 1920's but is now abandoned. It was once a pulp mill and a toilet paper manufacturing plant. Isn't this appropriate for their sacred place? Anyhow, the area around it is highly contaminated with industrial waste from many sources. This is why we went into the water near Safehaven District. It's not polluted there. I think we can slip in and out of their burrow without detection before Edward's Reconciliation herbs wear off.

Unfortunately, we are running out of time. Normally, I would honor our agreement to respect each other's sacred place but after tonight's event, I will count this as a tit for tat. Sid must know that even though we are a peaceful coven, aggression toward us will not be tolerated."

Emelie and Edward go off the trail again. We bushwhack to the water's edge then get onto an old dock made of aged and weathered wood. I'm startled by a noise. I realize we have disturbed a group of harbor seals sleeping on the dock. They hastily galumph to the edge of the dock and jump into the water making a splash. My adrenaline surges from the startle. I consciously try to calm myself.

I realize some people enjoy this feeling. They get stimulated by this kind of detail. Risk is exciting and energizing. These types tend to have a propensity for criminal behavior. It entertains them, makes them feel more alive and even normal. Thankfully I am not this type of person. Even though there is risk in my chosen profession, as a Private Investigator and former Police Officer, I feel normal without having to artificially raise my levels of adrenaline. I have met many officers that crave this type of stimulation. They are just on the opposite side of the law. An old police joke alleges the only difference between the police and the criminal is which side of the bars they are on. Although I have met many good officers, there are also the misguided ones.

I look up to see an old white smoke stack. It stands high and close to the bay. Nearby is a fenced-off lagoon holding stagnant, off-colored water. Large signs warn of hazardous wastes and say "Keep Out." The buildings are old and dilapidated. They are mostly made of old brick. Amongst the brick buildings stands one small wood building that doesn't seem to belong.

The buildings are boarded up and have signs saying they are condemned. We walk up to the tallest brick building. The door is partially open. Edward pushes on it to open it wider but the door sticks at a quarter open. Edward turns sideways and tightly passed through the doorway. We follow. The floor is made of cement that is covered in a thick layer of dirt. There are pools of brown water standing on the floors. As we progress through the building the ambient light gets dimmer. There are no windows on the ground floor but several stories up there are broken-out windows. In the center of the large building are long, oversized tanks. A draft comes from the broken windows above but barely turns the stagnant air. Edward takes out a crank flashlight, cranks it several times and the lens lights up. He points, "These were the wood chip tanks. Over there is the log chipper that cut the logs into chips for the tanks. The Digestion tanks are over there. This is where the chips where mixed with acid then heated to make pulp." Lexa comments, "I thought this was a haunted house."

I feel around and turn on the flashlight from my cell phone for more light. As I do this, I see what appears to be a large, dark rat run across my feet. I look at Harley and she makes an expression of disgust. Lexa lets out a high-pitched screech. Juni grabs an old straw broom, raises it above her head and chases after the rat. She stops abruptly as she runs out of the light provided by the flashlights. Lexa looks at her, "Now this is a cliché." Juni looks at the broom then jokingly puts it between her legs and acts as if she is flying. She makes a face at Lexa then rests the broom against some antiquated machinery.

Emelie points up to the ceiling. "Their space is up there. Even though these buildings have a view of the bay, the Darksider's like the view of downtown better. They find the tall buildings of the city more aesthetic than the water." We walk up an internal steel staircase that has little support except for one handrail. I try not to look down as I could easily slip and fall several stories. We carefully climb to the top story. The upper part of the north side of the building has fallen down. There are bricks from the outside structure lying on the floors inside, in disorganized piles. A large part of the roof is gone. The Darksiders have tables, couches and chairs, set out in an open floorplan. The furniture is placed under the remaining area of the roof at angles to prevent the rain from falling through the cavity onto the furniture. The living area looks like it could be from the latest issue of the most up-to-date architecture magazine. It utilizes covered space with open space, interior space with exterior space and a view of downtown. Emelie points, "This is Sid's area." There is a large bed with an elaborate carved, wooden headboard and footboard. The sheets on the mattress are made of fine linen and the bedspread is a red velvet. "This is where he entertains himself", Emelie adds sarcastically. The bed is unmade as if recently used. "There have always been questions about Sid's interests. He has always been a little different. When he was younger, he was always off to the side by himself on the playground, in the school lunchroom and at birthday parties. He spent most of his time by himself. As he grew older, he had more friends but his relationships seemed, unhealthy. He would either be in a care-taking role or a dependent, controlling role. The week before mother died, she told me that Sid had kissed her goodbye. At the time, I thought this was a surprisingly healthy behavior for Sid. But as mother went on to describe the kiss, it became apparent that Sid was confused about his relationship with his mother. Mom said Sid reminded her of a distant cousin who made her uncomfortable. This cousin was different as well. He would come to the house and hang around her but would never talk. She asked her grandmother about him. She told her to follow her gut and never be alone with him. Anyhow, mom said Sid had a similar feel to him. Mom admonished Sid for his inappropriateness toward her and he became enraged by her reaction."

As I scan over the living area, I see prescription drug bottles sitting on the nightstand. There is drug paraphernalia and pornographic magazines, along with leather harnesses and chains for bondage. I remind myself not to touch anything regardless of my curiosity. Who knows what they did with this stuff or where it has been. There is also magic paraphernalia such as a crystal skull, some candles and a black cape. To the side of the bed is a small terrarium with what looks like large cockroaches sitting on a small plant. The plant is yellowish and sick looking. Edward holds one of the leaves in his hand, examining it. "This plant is commonly known as Blue Sage, Firewood, Catnip or more commonly known as Weed. It is not close to the quality of my medicinal marijuana. It's like a sick cousin to my plants." Harley raises an eyebrow with interest.

Emelie hastily starts going through Sid's belongings. Lexa goes after her trying to straighten up, so it wouldn't be so obvious that someone was there. Lexa is organizing a pile of garments when she stops to look at a lacy item that catches her attention. She examines it, holding it up so she can see it better. It's a pair of lacy thong underwear. She gasps in revolt and tosses the underwear. They land on a lampshade and hang there.

Emelie desperately rummages through a wardrobe closet. She raises her line of vision to a shelf on the top of the closet. In the upper right side of the top shelf is a plastic grocery bag. She eagerly looks through the contents and takes out a small glass vessel of water. "This is our version of Holy Water. Water has the ability to hold energy. As you already know it is one of our main sources of power as white witches." She puts the vessel into her pocket. She pulls out a stone that is a beautiful blue-green and lavender-silver stone. As she turns the stone in the light, it changes colors.

"This is Labradorite Stone, like water, it holds energy. All stones have their own frequency of energy and therefore can be used for its' specific healing qualities. This stone is used for performing magic and awakening mystical, spiritual and psychic powers. It can quickly evoke significant changes in the one who uses it. It is a catalyst for serendipity and synchronicity. However, it has protective qualities, making it useless for dark magic. This won't be of use to Sid." Emelie puts it into her pocket. This stone is Rose Quartz. It is used for calming, restoring the blood and forgiveness. Sid may need this stone someday." Emelie puts the stone back into the plastic bag.

"Here are some roots used for healing. This is Ginseng. It has amazing qualities that energize, protect from stress and increase cognitive abilities. This is a turmeric root. This root is a powerhouse for healing. It has strong antioxidant qualities that are good for the immune system. It appears to impact cancer at all stages. It has been known to actually cure cancer but with varying results, as with all treatments, whether natural or traditional." Lexa repeats after Emelie "Tumor-ic." Emelie laughs and corrects her "Turmeric" but that is a good way of remembering its' use. Harley nods.

"Here are some cedar chips. Wood is also used for its magical qualities similar to the healing and magical qualities of plants. The Native American's call cedar their Tree of Life. Cedar can be used to make a wand; however, wands are not routinely used by the whitches but they are one of the tools we may use. Wands are used to focus energy. It's not the wand that is responsible for magic. It's the magical qualities of the wood and the powers of the whitch. These cedar chips are used to prepare a space for worship, summons the helpful spirits of our ancestors and clear negative energy."

"Here is what I came for. The amber necklace that was given to Sid as a first-degree apprentice." She pulls out the necklace from the bottom of the bag and slips it into her pocket with the Holy Water and the Labradorite stone. Emelie smiles mischievously. She puts the cedar chips into an ashtray then places her palm over the chips. They ignite causing a thin trail of white smoke that drifts upward. She blows on the smoke, dispersing the sweet cedar smell as she walks to each corner of the room. "There. Now the room is cleared from the negative energy of the Darksiders. This will hinder their black magic for a while." Emelie takes the smoking ashtray as she leads us out of the room. She clears the energy in all areas of the abandoned building before we exit.

I automatically squint as I step out of the old building into the light of the evening. Sam is waiting for me near the entrance. She jumps up and cat-walks her way to meet me. I look down to see a little rat where Sam was sitting. The rat lays motionless. Every once in a while, it makes a furtive movement to get away but Sam runs up to it and bats it down into submission. Sam just toys with it, grabbing it in her mouth and flipping it into the air. She chases after it and pounces on it when it tries to get away. This must be the same rat that ran across my path earlier. Sam appears proud of herself. She wants to show me she's a good hunter.

Emelie says, "You can communicate with Sam through your thoughts." I tell Sam, without speaking, to let the rat go because it may be someone's animal helper, like she is to me. Emelie coaches me. "Visualizing can be used in conjunction with talking to her. Visualization is quicker and clearer than using words. Animal friends seem to understand this easier." I visualized hugging her, feeling love for her and feeling full, not hungry, so Sam doesn't feel she needs to feed me. Sam drops the rat from her mouth. Initially the rat just lays there, expecting the cat to pounce once it tries to run away. Eventually the rat makes a move. Sam watches the rat with great discipline as it builds up speed then darts off, still expecting a chase. I hope the rat was a free agent and not a Darksider sympathizer. I visualize gratitude for Sam's actions. Sam starts purring loudly and rubs up against my leg. I pick her up and kiss the back of her head. I tuck her into my shirt. I visualize that I want her close to me and that we will have a long life together.

We walk back toward the old weathered dock. I visualize and tell the seals that we aren't there to hurt them. I get a feeling, a knowing, that the seals understand we have no ill intent and they needn't react to our presence. I get another message that there are others coming that they don't feel safe around. I look up toward the trail and see a group of people walking in our direction. This group has a dark energy. I look at Emelie. She nods, "I know." We divert our path and cut across to a trail further north. The Darksiders didn't seem aware of our presence. They are loud and intoxicated. "Powers are diminished with intoxication. I think we fooled them for now." I hear the seals plunge into the cool Baypoint Bay as the Darksiders get close. I don't recognize the members of this group. We turn and head toward campus, heading into the twilight.

Lawrence Anderson

Chapter 19

Free Delivery but No Returns

I'm eager to get back to the campus because I'm worried about Lawren and Luciana. I speed up my pace. We step onto the path that leads to Safehaven College. Unlike the walkways on main campus this path is dirt and lined with tall Evergreen trees. The dirt is cushioned by fir needles that have dried and fallen. There is a sweet sap smell that is released with each step. My heart is beating in my throat. I realize how dangerous Sid can be. My eyes are fixed in the direction of the lounge. From a distance, I can see Sid sitting on the couch in the lounge with Lawren and Luciana. He is sharing a flask with the two. As I get closer, I can see the flask has "Obsidian"

engraved into its stainless steel. Odious and Nefara are nowhere to be found.

The girls appear quite intoxicated. They laugh and engage with Sid. Sid appears sober except for the influence of the Reconciliation herbs. He is staring intently at Lawren. She is sharing memories of law school and he, in turn, talks about his doctorate program. They don't seem to notice we are there. I stop to think about how they could make a powerful couple with his Ph. D in Business and her law degree. I try to think fewer disturbing thoughts but realize she would be related to me by marriage. To be exact, she would be my step aunt. What a dark thought. She would be my new dark aunt/former friend and classmate, who married my evil uncle. Definitely a mismatch. I shake my head and try to shake off these thoughts but they just keep popping into my head. Certainly, this would improve his gene pool. Lawren has such beautiful features in contrast to Sid's. She also has a better personality as well. How stereotypical for a professor to date a younger woman. I focus harder on halting this train of thought, as I just can't tolerate it any longer.

Finally, Sid looks up. "Oh, Andi. How are you? Emelie and Edward, my wonderful siblings. And the rest of your friends." He her returns his attention to Lawren and continues to smile. My train of thoughts start again. At least their union may reconcile the Darksiders and the whitches. Sid invites us, "Have a seat. We are sharing old memories. This has really been a quite pleasurable evening. We should do this more often."

Sid takes Lawren's hand and holds it for some time. I gesture to Lawren to take her hand back but I think she is too drunk. He comments "Your hands are so soft and warm." Lawren looks up at Sid. Her eyes appear slightly crossed. I turn sideways and wedge my body between the two, breaking Sid's grip from Lawren's hand. Sid and Lawren slide to opposite ends of the couch, giving me room between them.

I say "Lawren has had too much to drink." I force the flask out of her hand as she is bringing it to her mouth. Luciana is trying not to smile but the corners of her mouth turn upwards. She lets out a giggle then tries to stifle it. "It's time we get these girls back." I set down the flask and grab their hands, pulling them up. Sid appears disappointed. He looks at Emelie. "Deep down inside, sister, I long to be part of the coven." Emelie looks surprised when he says this. She subconsciously checks her pocket to see if the talisman is still there. "Well then, one more drink before I return to my den." Sid takes a long swig from the flask, finishing off the remaining alcohol. He stands up to leave but quickly sits back down again. He stares straight ahead then falls backwards. He appears to drift into a deep sleep. I look at Edward in amazement. "What happened?" Edward appears amused. "My sleeping herbs work. I also added a couple of other herbs to take away his memory. He will wake up and believe he passed out from too much alcohol, not remembering much of anything at all." Lawren and Luciana look at each other and start laughing. They try to hug each other but miss then tumble drunkenly onto the couch. It seems they need a little time to sober up. I search for some coffee but all I can find is a bag of Bugles. I throw the bag at Lawren but her reaction time is slow. The bag hits her in the face. Slowly she picks up the bag and somehow is able to rip it open. Little horn shaped corn snacks fly into the air. Lawren picks up five corn horns and puts one on each finger of her hand. She proceeds to eat one at a time working her way from her thumb toward her pinky finger. Luciana leans over and bites into the last one on her pinky before Lawren can. They both start laughing again. Sid starts snoring loudly. Luciana puts two Bugles on either side of his head pointing upward. They look like devil horns. She laughs even harder. She tries to balance them so they will sit without being held but they keep falling. She gives up and decides to turn them around and wedge them up his nose. His snoring becomes louder. I ask where Odious and Nefara are. Lawren and Luciana reply in unison. "They went to get popcorn, cocoa and board games."

I hear honking outside on the patio. I run out to the patio. Edward and Emelie are sitting in a 1941 red Chevy pickup. Edward backs in facing the bed toward the lounge. He puts it in neutral and jumps out. Emelie runs after him. I follow the two. He and Emelie grab Sid. Harley, Lexa and Juni take the remaining extremities and lift him. I run ahead to open the tailgate. Sid is roughly tossed into the bed of the truck. Harley, Lexa and Juni jump into the bed with Sid. I run back into the lounge and gather Lawren and Luciana. They are now talking with Bugles in their mouth, spraying dry crumbs everywhere and then laughing. I grab both of them, march them out to the truck, guide them into the bed and close the tailgate. I jump in. Emelie opens the slider window between the cab and the bed. The song Summertime by Janis Joplin is playing on the vintage radio. "Summertime, time, time" Janis screams out, hitting every note in a raw, emotional narration. "One of these mornings you're going to rise, rise up singing. You're gonna spread your wings, child. And take to the sky." Lawren and Luciana are moving to the music in a demonstrative way. Lawren tells Edward to turn it up. The rest of us start moving to the music and singing along. I recognize the station as the student radio station at Wasgard. I'm so much in the moment due to the summer evening, the fresh air, good friends, good music and the wind in my face, that I forget the task at hand. I come back to reality as a scarf flies out of the cab and hits me in the face. Emelie throws out more scarves for the others. Emelie gestures over the music to use the scarves to wrap up our hair. She also throws out a blanket.

Edward heads toward the Safehaven District. When we get to Maritime Drive, he takes a right and heads toward downtown. It is dusk. The sky is beautiful with clouds and the last glimpse of the summer sun at the horizon. I feel a rush as Edward accelerates. Lawren and Luciana are hanging their heads over the side of the truck enjoying the sensation of the wind in their drunken state. Juni grabs Lawren and Harley grabs Luciana to pull them back into the bed to keep them from falling out. I wonder how they are going to feel tomorrow.

I notice a late model, black convertible, sport car approaching from behind. It's coming at a high rate of speed. It catches up to us then tailgates. The license plate has the word "ObSIDyn" on it. Odious and Nefara are in the front seats. They don't seem to recognize us with the scarves on. Luciana and Lawren are too drunk to put their scarves on but the wind is blowing their hair in their face. Edward slows down to allow Odious to pass, hoping they will not recognize us and be on their way. I turn my head away, trying to be inconspicuous. Luciana notices the rude driver passing too close and too fast. She leans out further from the bed almost touching their car and flips them off. The sport car decelerates briefly, as if to consider stopping to confront us. I grab Luciana's birdy finger, pull her hand down and her body back into the bed. All we need is an incident of road rage. Lawren leans over, waves and smiles pretentiously as the wind blows her hair out of her face. I hurriedly grab a scarf and wrap her hair and face. The rest of the us, the sober ones, also wave in a friendly manner. The sport car speeds up again and gains distance. Nefara throws several items out of the car window and onto the side of the street. The sports car continues to speed toward downtown, in the direction of the old paper mill, its taillights disappear in the distance. I let out a sigh of relief then look down at Sid passed out in the bed of the truck. I say "Nice car." Of course, he cannot hear me. He still has Bugles sticking out his nose. I note that he looks like a nicer person when he is sleeping.

Edward slows down briefly. I look over the bed to see what was thrown out to the side of the street. There is a newly purchased board game, cocoa and popcorn. I guess the spell must have ran its course. It appears that Odious and Nefara no longer want to play.

We take a left toward the water into a residential neighborhood then drive down a long driveway. The home at the end of the driveway is large, of modern architectural design and made of various natural materials such as metal and stone. It's facing west toward the bay but there are only inconsequential windows on the bay view side. The siding is an unusual dark slate. The fence is also made of the same material with large, square columns that appear regularly throughout its lengths connected with wrought iron. These columns have the design on them of a dark square with a flame which is engraved in the slate. It's obvious this home is unique or more accurately, unusual, in comparison to the other homes in the neighborhood. It gives an impression that the homeowner is a little eccentric. There are no lights on in the house. It looks dark and cold. "Where are we?" I ask. Lawren becomes lucid for a moment and says, "This is Sid's house."

The old red Chevy comes to a stop with a slight squeaking noise from the brakes. The house is enclosed by the stone fence, so it is impossible for Edward to get closer to the house with the truck. Edward and Emelie get out and walk back to the bed of the truck. Emelie announces, "We have to carry him." Edward opens the tailgate and takes one of Sid's feet in each hand and tugs, pulling him to the edge of the open tailgate. Sid rolls his head to the side and makes a groaning noise. I jump up and grab his arm, directing the others to help lift him out of the truck before he wakes up. He is heavier than he looks.

We strenuously lift him out of the bed. I look at Lexa and recognize the face she is making. I've seen it before, especially in stressful situations or when dark magic is involved. She grabs her gut but then realizes releasing Sid causes a change in his weight distribution. Sid's hip dips down and the others grunt with the additional weight. Lexa puts her hand back under Sid to equalize the distribution but she quickly draws it back again grabbing her gut. The others grunt due to the lack of equilibrium then look at Lexa in a perturbed manner. Lexa blurts out, "I guess I'm not the only one who has to use the bathroom. I think he peed himself." The others look down and sneer. We walk faster in hopes to dump him off faster. Emelie steps in front of us as we are shuffling toward the wrought iron gate. She holds her hand up to stop us. More groans linger in the air.

Emelie turns to the house and makes symbols with her hand. She addressed the four corners. Edward hands her a woven stick of herbs. Emelie places it above her open palm. Instantaneously the stick starts to smolder, letting off a sweet, grassy smell. She waves the smoldering stick toward the north, south, east and west. She points it up to the sky then downward at the ground. She puts the lit stick in her mouth and grabs Sid again. The iron gate squeaks as it opens. I hope the noise doesn't draw attention to us. We rush toward the front porch, up the stone steps, near the front door. Emelie waves the smudge stick around the porch then tries the door. It is locked. The porch is semi-enclosed. "This will have to do." "He will be uncomfortable and probably stiff when he wakes but he will be safe." Edward counts, "one, two." Lexa drops Sid on the count of two instead of three, causing him to slip out of our grip. He bangs his head as his dead-weight hits the ground. We stand and stare at Lexa in disappointment.

Lexa wipes her hands in a symbolic gesture of being done with the task. She smiles with satisfaction for a moment then frantically runs back to the truck. We join Lawren and Luciana in the bed. They are leaning against each other sleeping. Emelie and Edward jump into the cab. The truck starts instantaneously. The radio is now playing Carly Simon's Legend in Your Own Time. No one sings. I just listen to the lyrics quietly.

"Well I have known you. Since you were a small boy. And your mama used to say My boy is gonna grow up and be Some kind of leader someday. Then you'd turn on the radio And sing with the singer in the band. Your mama would say to you This isn't exactly what we had planned. But you are a legend in your own time.

A hero in the footlights. Playing tunes to fit your rhyme But the legend's only a lonely boy. When he goes home alone."

I look back to see Sid lying on his front porch, alone in the dark, wet with urine and realize how fitting this song is.

Edward slowly drives away without turning on his headlights. He carefully drives several blocks before turning them on. I see an outline of a deer standing off to the side as the headlights light up the road. I tap on Juni's shoulder and point at the deer. She softly calls out to the doe and smiles. Edward continues to drive slowly toward Safehaven College at a speed the deer can follow.

Chapter 20

Whitch runs in the Family

We dress in our robes, put on our amber necklaces and light our candles to make the trek to The Tree of Life. This is our last night at Safehaven. There will be a ceremony to celebrate our recent accomplishments and to cleanse our mind and body. The trail is pitch black outside of the candle's light. It is unusually quiet. We softly sing and meditate as we climb Conundrum Hill. The moon is bright. There is a faint smell of scented candles in the air. Our animal friend's walk in front, to the side and behind us, with the exception of Sam, who is tucked inside my robe.

The Tree is beautiful in the moonlight. Emelie and Edward direct us to the side of the tree between the pond. We place our candles at the four corners. Emelie opens our sacred space by acknowledging our ancestors, inviting them to be present and give us guidance. She makes symbols in the air with her finger. We take off our shoes, then our robes leaving on our ceremonial undergarments. I gradually wade down into the pond. The water is surprisingly warm and relaxing. Immediately I feel the energy from the water come up through my feet and replenish my body. I feel an energy come down from the sky into the crown of my head and descend down my back. The stress from the day melts away.

Emelie speaks. "This is similar to the cleansing rituals of other cultures throughout time. These ceremonies were used especially for warriors after they returned from battle. Though our battle was not violent, it was still a battle. What we did today is a turning point in the balance of power between the light and dark forces. Now we celebrate our accomplishments but with caution, as there will likely be other battles ahead."

The energy in the pond continues to accumulate and move in the current. I can see different colors moving in various patterns as I look down into the water. These colors represent the colors of the rainbow. I feel a presence and connection to all living things. My mind drifts between past, present and future. The energy force penetrates deep into my body. It heals and replenishes. It is palatable and ethereal.

I close my eyes and this presence becomes more intense. I see images behind my closed eyelids and my head starts to swirl a bit. I see and hear Lady Madsen and hear other voices echoing with hers. She says, "There is no such thing as reincarnation. It is rightfully called renewal. All things are recycled in a way that brings them back into existence but in a renewed state. The universe, the stars, the world, people, animals, microorganisms, atoms, subatomic particles, all work according to this pattern. What happens on earth, happens in a cell. What is on earth is also in heaven. Do not be afraid of these patterns. They are part of you and you part of them. And so, it is, my granddaughter, Orenda."

I feel a healing energy in every cell and an overwhelming sensation of love both inside and outside of my body. I feel rested, as if I just took a fresh breath of air or woke up from a nap. My thoughts

Hans C Anderson

are calm and pure. My body is relaxed and replenished. So, this is what Emelie was talking about?

We are quiet for a while soaking in this energy. Emelie speaks again. "The amber necklace with the coyote fur is safe. Once we are whitches, we are always whitches, until we return our amber necklace and retire our craft name. Now I have Sid's amber necklace and it is rightly returned to the whitches. It is official."

Edward opens up some pear cider. The cork pops and flies approximately ten feet. Bubbles flow over the lip of the long necked, green glass bottle. We hold our ceremonial chalices under the bottle trying to recover the natural effervescence. Once the flow of foam stops, Edward fills each chalice. We toast and drink in the floral and pineapple undertones. I look up at the stars. I want to remember this moment. There are certain times when everything feels perfect. The combination of feeling satisfied by accomplishment, being with my friends, my new-found family, my ancestors, being beneath this beautiful tree, in this pool of viable water, under the warm summer night sky and drinking the most perfect, homemade, pear cider. What could make this better? I look at the branches of the tree in the starlight. I notice two big, bright, yellow eyes looking back at me from inside the branches. It feels like I was looking back at myself. I guess I answered my own question. My new animal companion, Sam. I feel an old familiarity, like we have walked together before. I repeat to myself, what could make this better? Just then, I hear a ringtone of a cell phone. Quickly I turn to my pack and grab my cell phone. There hasn't been any reception since we arrived. I answer. "Hi mom. We're doing fine. When are you coming home? We miss you." My heart melts. The voice of my oldest daughter Channon. I repeat to myself. What could make this better? "Hi mom" The voice of Kaite Lynn is heard in the background. I realize how much I miss them. "Is aunt Kristine taking good care of you?" "Yes mom", they say in unison. "But we miss you. When are you coming home?" "Tomorrow. Everything I needed to do is done here. Guess what? I found out we have family here that I didn't know about. I met my aunt and uncle or your great aunt and great uncle. I want you to meet them." At this point, I switch to speaker phone so that Emelie and Edward can hear the voices of their nieces.

"Well, mom, something unusual happened a couple of days ago. A dog just showed up on our back porch. We kept the gate locked as you told us, so I am not sure how he got into our backyard. He is laying on our porch and does not seem to want to leave. He acts like he is at home. He looks skinny, so we're feeding him cheese and apples. It gives him terrible gas but we don't have any dog food. Aunt Kristine says he is an English Bulldog. Can we keep him?" I say, "I don't know but we will talk about it when I get home. A dog like that must have an owner." I wanted to tell them about Sam but I decided to let it be a surprise when I get home. "Is everything else okay?" I ask. Channon talks over Kaite Lynn. "Kaite has been talking in her sleep. I can tell she is dreaming. She keeps repeating the name, Amrita. I think she has been watching too many fantasy movies."

I look at Emelie and Edward as they are listening. They stare at each other after Channon says this. "Okay you two. Tell my sister I say hi and give her a big hug for me. Don't forget to eat well and don't let the dog in the house. Love you and no more fantasy movies. See you tomorrow." "We love you too. Say hi to our new aunt and uncle. Tell them we look forward to meeting them." Emelie and Edward say good-bye and promise to call soon.

I end the call. "Wow that is weird. I have been trying to get reception ever since I got here, then all of the sudden." I stop and look intensely at Emelie and Edward due to the unusual look on their faces. Emelie speaks slowly, "Andi, your grandmother's craft name is Amrita." I drop the cell phone. "This is an indication that Kaite Lynn and possibly even Channon, may have communications with our ancestors and special relationships with animals. These are common signs of magical abilities." I look down to see the colors in the pond swirling energetically. I'm happy that I may be able to share my new life with my daughters but I'm also nervous about how to explain this new world with all of its potential risks and opportunities.

The other whitches from the coven start to gather. They stand shoulder to shoulder in a circle around the pond. They look spectacular in their ceremonial robes and veils while holding their lit candles. I am looking forward to a night of singing, dancing and celebration with my sisters and brothers.

Chapter 21

So Many Things

The dorm is warm and cozy. I stretch then roll over in my twin bed to see Harley staring at me. "Everyone else is already awake. We are waiting for you to come to breakfast at the pharm. Edward has made sorghum and Hopi Blue corn pancakes over the fire. The coffee is percolating." She throws my favorite shirt at me and kicks my shoes that are lying on the floor toward my feet. Slowly I get out of bed and start dressing. Harley pushes me from behind toward the door to the hallway.

It's a warm morning. I have to close my eyes as I walk out into the bright sun. The air is fresh and I can smell eggs and pancakes cooking over the fire. I feel rejuvenated like I have slept sixteen restful hours. My body is light, energetic and my mind clear. I turn around to see Sam running up behind me.

I grab a blue enamel cup and pour some dark coffee into it. I need to use a pot holder because the coffee pot is so hot from the fire. Edward has buried some potatoes wrapped in banana leaves in the coals next to the fire. My mouth starts to water. Edward hands me a plate of steaming food. I pour some maple syrup over my plump stack of pancakes and cut into them with a fork. "Hey Edward, where did you get this maple syrup? It has amazing flavor." Edward smiles. "It is part of my experiment. I have many plant trials going on. I am working on plants that grow in the winter, plants that don't need much water, plants that don't need light and Maple trees that bear maple syrup all year long." I ask, "Did you grow this coffee here?" Edward smirks coyishly.

"Juni has a surprise for us" I grab my plate and coffee and follow the group to the Safehaven Lounge where a drum circle is waiting. I laugh and exclaim, "My favorite activity." Juni smiles, "I want you to drum along with me. I wrote a song for my best friends and new family." Juni sits at the piano and starts playing. She smiles and bears down on the keys creating unique chords and rhythms. We start drumming deliberately trying to learn the melody. Lexa is her typical off-beat, out of rhythm, self. She is concentrating hard but continues drum in a disorganized pattern. I laugh as the tempo rises and falls.

Juni announces in a microphone, "This song is called A Whitches Song." She begins to sing in perfect pitch.

"Flying through the night. Is she black or is she white?" Juni adds a musical ditty and continues, "Is her magic doing good? Is she evil or just misunderstood?"

"Her silhouette against the moon. Flying high upon her broom. Is she a hero or our doom? Either way we will know soon."

"Okay whitches sing the chorus with me." We sing along, "Which witch is she? Is she a whitch like me? Why can't I see? Is she a whitch like me?"

I look around to see Emelie banging on her drum. Edward is laughing and smiling as he watches her play. Harley is stomping her feet to the beat and cheering Juni on. Luciana and Lawren are not sure about our ritual but play along in a reserved fashion. Juni starts singing again after a lengthy instrumental on the piano;

"Is she going to enlighten you or poison you with her witch's brew? Is she one of my kind? Is she evil or divine? What the hell is on her mind? Treachery or Salvation?

"Always seen with her cat and her big black pointed hat." I point to Sam. "Do I really look like that? Are we both the same or do we only share the name?"

We join in singing the chorus:

"Which witch is she? Is she a whitch like me? Why can't I see? Is she a whitch like me?"

We look at each other and gesture as if we are asking a question to the person across the circle. We return to drumming again.

"Is her skin youthful or green? Is she a savior or a fen? Is she scary or just a good fairy? Is she giving good advice or simply looking for a sacrifice? "

"Pointed shoes and pointed nose. Into the night where does she go? Laughing loudly through the dewy mist. Is she a disaster or a gift?"

We all sing, "Which witch is she? Is she a whitch like me? Why can't I see? Is she a whitch like me?

"Does she like her coven? Or is she putting the neighbor's children in the oven? Does she align with the devil or God? Is she friendly or just a fraud? Does she prowl into the night? Turning her face away from the light. Do we share the same plight? Is she a whitch like me?"

"Is she sexy or scary? Fishnet stockings or are her legs hairy? Or is she a beauty queen? Black high heels, high cut skirt, wicked eyes that tease and flirt. Is she the answer to my dream or a twisted evil queen?"

"Should I know her? Join forces and adore her? Please mirror, mirror show me the future. Is she a whitch like me? As I wish at the wishing well. Is she from Heaven or does she belong to Hell? Only good time will tell. Is she a whitch like me?"

Juni prompts, "Okay one last chorus."

"Which witch is she? Is she a whitch like me? Does she share my history? Is she a whitch like me?"

As we finish up the song. It dawns on me. Juni sings and plays piano like a professional. I remember what Lawren told me the night of our initiation ceremony. The anonymous performer on campus wore a robe and veil throughout her performance. Lawren also said that the performance started very late that night. This would give a whitch at the initiation time to go to both events. "Which witch is she? Is she a witch like Juni?" I say to myself. I look over at Lawren then look at Juni. I guess I could also say the same thing about Lawren. "Which whitch is she?" She has been on both sides, the Darksiders and the Whitches. She has spent time at Sid's home and Sid clearly has affection for her.

The others are clapping and laughing. I turn my attention toward the circle. Juni starts on another song. Her melodic voice and perfect piano. Edward pops a cork from a bottle of kombucha. He pours it into glasses that are lined up in a row. The viscous liquid bubbles up, over the glasses and onto the table. The content is amber, full bodied and effervescent. Edward leads a toast. "To my new family. What is mine is yours. You are always welcome. Besides, I always need help on the pharm." We raise our glasses and clink, spilling kombucha. Luciana looks a little sick. "This reminds me too much of yesterday. I'm still a little hungover." She clanks her glass on Lawren's. Both Luciana and Lawren take very small sips. Luciana muffles a gag as she tries to swallow. Lawren looks at her empathetically then forcibly swallows, starts gagging and runs for garbage can.

Emelie clears her throat to make an announcement. "To the apprentice whitches. Next season you will become a second degree whitch and get the trunk of your tree tattooed on the base of your neck. Always keep your amber necklace close. This is your coven membership. And always keep your craft name secret. This is the name only your coven will call you. Losing either of these makes you vulnerable. Always care for your animal helper. You are here for them and they for you. Remember, whitches first, community second, always do good, always bring light, build an honorable legacy, love one another and care for The Tree of Life. Our coven relies on Sanctity, Secrecy and Service. Go forth into the world but always come back to the coven. May you be safe in your travels and may we meet again soon." The bubbles tickle my throat and my nose. The flavor lingers in my palate.

I look over at Emelie. She has tears in her eyes. She walks over and grabs my hand. She pulls me close and hugs me tight. As she holds me, she whispers in my ear. "I am so glad we have reunited. I have missed you and never want to be separated again. You have grown to be a beautiful and caring person. I see your mother in you. You are always welcome here with me, to help me govern the coven. You could work for the campus police. We have friends here. This would also make Edward happy. He is very fond of you. I want to meet my nieces. I miss my family." Emelie kisses my cheek. "You are like your mother. She would be very proud of you also. The offer is always open. I love you, my dear."

Edward hands me sacred, dried pears, homemade cookies and a small bottle of kombucha. "These are for the road. The cookies are chocolate chip and pecan. I made them for my nieces. Oh, and here." He hands me some left-over scrambled eggs. "These are for Sam. She loves eggs." I hug him tight. He smells fresh like nature. I breathe in. "Hmmm, Sandalwood?" He replies, "Yes, how did you know?" "I was a Safehaven student, remember?" "Oh yeah, one of the ten essentials for Safehaven students." "I haven't used it for a while. It brings back good memories. Thanks for the food. I will tell your nieces about you. You will meet them soon."

Lexa is doing a solo on her drum. Juni is trying jump in with the piano but is unable to due to the irregularity of Lexa's beat. The others are smirking and laughing. I notice Harley is not in the circle.

I look for her on the patio. She is sitting by the pond. As I walk up to her, I instantly recognized the scent. Harley is trying to conceal what is in her hand. Once she realizes she is busted, she brings her hand up with a rolled joint in it.

"Don't tell Edward. I stumbled upon his medicinal crop this morning before breakfast. This is the best marijuana I have ever smoked. Less potent but very sweet and smooth. I took a little extra to press for oil. I am curious about the oils medicinal value. I have some very sick patients at my practice. I have to sample the product, you know?"

"I know, Harley. And knowing Edward, I am sure it's nothing but the highest quality of organic, heritage cannabis. He is a master gardener."

"Yeah, I have to stop smoking. I need to shed some of these destructive habits. I feel this experience has changed me. I don't feel as compulsive about my bad habits as I used to. Here, do you want to try it?"

"No, after all the years in law enforcement, using drugs is not in my constitution. Have you ever thought about leaving Seattle and moving back to Baypoint? I miss it here. Deep inside I feel this is my home. For years, I have had recurrent dreams that I am living in Baypoint. This is the place where I was so happy as a student. In my dreams, I cry because I am so happy to be back. It's always so magical here. You know, college, this beautiful place, my friends, our professors, learning about life and so much more. Back then, it was just perfect. Why did we ever leave? Now, I know why this is such a magical place. There is magic afoot." I tickle Harley as I say this. Harley starts singing "Which whitch is she? Is she a whitch like me?" She puts her joint out and puts her arm around me. Together we walk across the patio back to the lounge.

Lawren exclaims, "There you two are. We wondered where you were. I think Juni and Lexa should go on tour." I smile and wink at Juni. Juni looks at me in a knowing way. "I think this would be a good idea." I look at Lexa, "I think you have missed your calling."

Lexa changes the subject, "Speaking of which, Luciana informed me that there is a coaching position open for the basketball team. I think I still have some things I can teach the young women. But you can relax, I won't neglect my musical talent." "That's good. You should not deprive the world of your Goddess given abilities." I goad.

Emelie stands up to speak. I ask Lawren to get my phone to take a picture of all of us before we leave. "I think my phone is in the dorm room"

Emilie waits for Lawren to leave. "Luciana is pledging to our coven." I turn in surprise, as Luciana announces. "It's not official yet. I am too busy to enter an apprenticeship program now but I will be joining your forces and starting my apprentice studies next summer. I have also decided to partner with Dania in the Physics Department. This will keep me very busy until then. We will be working on a project that researches the energetic fields outside our bodies and how these fields effect matter inside and outside our bodies, to include our genetic code. I'm so excited." I ask, "So, what is Eric doing since the break-up of your partnership?" "He is going to continue his search for the fountain of youth. I don't think he has an option. He's in deep with Sid and his cronies. Apparently, the Business Department has found a very supportive multi-national corporation to fund his project. Maybe he will also discover a way to heal Sid's limp. Either one of these discoveries will save his head." There is sarcasm in her tone. Emelie announces that Edward was offered the contract for Food Services on campus. I clap and to congratulate him. "Say goodbye to gastro distress across the campus. The university will save thousands of dollars in toilet paper."

Lawren comes back saying she could not find my phone. Then excuses herself to go to the bathroom. Emelie directs her upstairs to the bathroom near the cafeteria. "It is the only bathroom open." As she walks toward the stairway, Luciana reminds Lawren that they have to leave soon so she can drop her off at the airport in time for her flight back to California. Lawren waves, acknowledging these plans, without turning around. She walks briskly toward the bathroom.

"Should we convoy to Seattle?" I ask Harley, Lexa and Juni. "Why don't we follow each other. Just in case someone has car trouble. Next year we can carpool here. That is if we are still living in the Seattle area." "Yeah", Juni sighs. "There are many reasons to move this way. Things have changed since this weekend." I interject, "You know when you think that you have everything figured out, such as your career, where to raise your family or where to grow old and retire, suddenly something happens that you never expected and your world turns upside down. Nothing is the same and it will never be the same. You have to react to the situation because you have also changed. The funny thing is when I was younger and thought about my life in the future, all of this was never in my consciousness. It is a surprise how things actually turn out. Fate can be influenced by many things, such as past decisions, your career, who you marry, or not, kids and where you find a job. Then an unknown happens. Something not even likely to happen and your life goes off in another direction. Luckily our life-changing experience isn't negative. Never the less, our lives have changed and there is no turning back. It will be interesting to try and settle back into our regular routine, like we used to."

Harley looks concerned. "What if I can't control my magic?" Lexa agrees and adds "What if I accidentally change the future due to just a casual thought? This could be a serious matter. Except if it is winning the Lottery. That would be okay. Just think, I could buy a house in a rich neighborhood. Maybe one next to Sid, here in Baypoint, get a sleek black sports car, an entourage...." She chuckles.

Emelie and Edward are sitting back listening then stand holding old journals, books and loose papers. Emilie announces. "These were former apprentices' study materials. They are passed down from the fourth- degree whitches to the new apprentices." Emelie and Edward distribute these materials. Emelie hands me several items. "These were your mother's. I've been holding on to them for decades. Lillie, I mean your mother, Lilith, devoured this material. She went through all four degrees in record time. I don't think anyone has done it in less time. Your mother was so gifted. She was assumed to be the next high priestess but then she just disappeared. She left her job, her family and the coven hanging. No explanation. No note explaining anything. We didn't suspect foul play because she took actions such as withdrawing money from the bank, buying large amounts of groceries for the family and packing luggage. She even took time to resign her position at work. Her disappearance appeared to be carefully planned and her whereabouts covered up. Never the less, I miss her. It was tough on your father but Miron stepped up and raised you kids. You turned out wonderfully. How is your father anyway?"

I take a moment to reply as I am still in shock from the new information I just obtained about my mother. "Oh, dad is traveling. He lives in the city next to me, Fir View but travels frequently due to work. I'm not sure where he is now but he was recently in California. He travels up and down the West Coast, including Canada."

Emelie smiles. "I'm glad he is doing well and staying active. Did

he ever remarry?" "No, he seemed too busy and not interested. He spent all of his spare time with us kids. He hasn't dated since mom left but has always been happy." "Very well then" says Emelie. Edward appears interested in the family history and is listening attentively.

I tightly grip the materials in my arms. There are books and journals of different sizes, colors and weights. They are heavy and awkward. Some loose papers fall out of my arms. Edward picks them up and hands them back to me. I can't wait to dive into this material. I notice handwritten notes. I haven't seen my mother's handwriting since I was a kid.

Emelie places her hand on my shoulder. "I just grabbed the bundle. You can go through it. I don't even know what is there." "Well, thank you aunt Em. I mean Emelie." This sounded awkward and felt uncomfortable. Emelie pulls me close to her, hugging me again and brushes her hand through my hair. Edward places his hand on my back. I start tearing up. Good-byes can be so stressful. I look around at the others. They also look like they are about to cry.

Lawren returns from the bathroom. "I'm next", I say. "It is a long drive home." I quickly run up the stairs. I had business to do. Not the usual business people due in the bathroom. I walk through the cafeteria, down the hall and into the bathroom. I open the stall door, turn around and sit down on the toilet. I look at the door in front of me. I take out a felt pen and lean forward. It's as if I'm channeling Joan of Arch. I write in purple ink, "I am the drum on which God is beating out his message." I look at what I just wrote and change the word God to God(dess) and the word his to his/her. I look at it but it looks incomplete. Another quote comes into my head. "I am not afraid. I was born to do this." I smile and say to myself, "My sentiment exactly."

I'm quickly distracted by some light blue ink that was not there last Friday. It says "Life is an unfoldment, and the further we travel, the more truth we can comprehend. To understand the things that are at our door is the best preparation for understanding those that lie beyond. --Hypatia."

As I scan the other walls of the stall, I see other new quotes in various colors of ink. This one is in magenta, "Are you a good witch or a bad witch?.....You've always had the power my dear, you just had to learn it for yourself. -- Gilda, the good witch of the North from the Wizard of Oz"

In teal ink, "Sometimes, it's easier to be led than lead. And a great many of our citizens prefer to stand on the sidelines and ignore their rights instead of defend them. They're called The Silent Majority" and "Now when it comes to Santa Claus, most mortals don't believe he exists...Just like they don't believe in witches. --Samantha from the TV show Bewitched"

I laugh out loud and feel grateful that my alumni friends are keeping the tradition of political bathroom graffiti alive. Definitely, there is a whitch theme to these new quotes.

I finish up with my other business. I pull some toilet paper off the roll to wipe. I look down at the floor to see a piece of paper has fallen away from the other group of material Emelie gave me. It is written in my mother's handwriting. I examine it for a minute. I lift my pen and write "There is so much free energy in the world. Just think if you could harness it then direct it in a positive way for the benefit of others?" I write the author's name mindfully, --"My mother, Lilith."

New Possibilities and Sad Good-byes

The others have migrated to the patio and continue the long process of saying good-bye. Edward and Emelie are handing out Safehaven College sweatshirts as going-away presents. We put them on over our existing shirts and wear them proudly. Our animal familiars have also gathered outside. They seem to sense a shift in our mood and know change is about to take place. They are gathered in a semi-circle at the periphery of the patio and carefully watch us to see what will happen. I scoop up Sam. I can sense her tension and uneasiness. Susy, the pig, is running up behind Lexa with her nose down toward the ground. When Lexa turns around the pig circles her then runs back to the periphery. Lexa encourages Susy to come up to her but Susy remains timid and unsure. The doe trots to the side of the patio then jumps onto the hillside above the patio.

Edward hands Harley a woven nest made out of twigs, leaves and other plant fibers. Harley takes it and pulls on each side of it with her hands. She notices that the sides of the nest are elastic and flexible. Edward tells her the nest is bound together using spider silk. Harley recognizes the high-pitched hum and looks up to see her hummingbird darting around above her. The goat and fox are also standing by but don't seem as anxious as the other animals.

Edward talks to the group. "By the way, I wanted everyone to know that late last night I went to the Ancient Library and sifted through some of the older books. I read a book on some of the original grafting techniques used on The Tree of Life hundreds of years ago. When I woke up this morning, I headed up Conundrum Hill to try out some of the techniques. I grafted the branch that Sid cut off back onto the tree. That and a touch of magic, it seems like it is going to take. It was important for me to try to restore our tree back to her original form. I couldn't allow Sid to defile her. Hopefully buds will form on the branches this fall and there will be fruit next Summer." Clapping breaks out amongst us.

I noticed just prior to this announcement that Lawren quickly left the group and ran up the stairs toward the bathroom again. She looked pale. I head up the stairs to check on her. I throw the bathroom door open and scan under the stalls for a set of feet. Instead, I find her crumpled, in front of the base of the toilet. I call out for help. I grab Lawren's head and cradle it. Sweat beads on her forehead and her shirt is drenched with sweat. She is shivering. "Are you okay, Lawren?" She groans in a low and labored tone. Emelie and the others run into the bathroom. Emelie grabs her wrist, feels her pulse and touches various places on her body. She appears to be doing some type of exam. She looks at Lawren's tongue. I look, in concern, at Emelie, hoping she can answer some questions. "Well Lawren, you are either suffering from complications of a hangover or, you are replete."

Lexa reaches into her pants pocket and pulls out a half-eaten granola bar. "Here, this will make you feel better since you Need to Eat." Lawren looks at the bar and turns a light shade of green. Emelie tells Lexa, "I didn't say she needs to eat." Lexa looks at her and says, "I think she is trying to be Discreet that's why she came up here to be all by herself." Emelie corrects her, not "discreet." Lexa looks puzzled, "Yeah she does look Downbeat. This is a good place to Retreat and Excrete what's making you sick. You did Mistreat yourself last night. Quite a lot to drink for your Petite size. We all stare at Lexa. "I guess this exercise has become Obsolete." Lexa appears frazzled and realizes she is not getting any closer to what Emelie was trying to say. Lexa squeezes out a last comment, "At least you are not Incomplete. You have all of us." Emelie sighs "I didn't say incomplete."

Emelie appears exasperated. "Late. Carrying cargo. In a family way. A Bun in the Oven. Mother to be." Lexa reaches into her pocket and pulls out the other half of the unwrapped granola bar and says "Here is the other half since you are eating for two." We turn our attention from Lexa to Lawren.

Lawren moans, "I can't be pregnant. I haven't been with anyone." Lexa shrugs, smiles, takes some fuzz off the unwrapped bar and puts it in her mouth with satisfaction. Lawren mumbles "Though, I have been nauseated in the mornings and I feel like I have gained some weight." She laughs to herself in a miserable way. "The only man I've been around is my father, Edward, uh, Odious and Sid. Therefore, it must be a hangover."

Emelie presses her index and middle finger on the inside of Lawren's inner forearm, approximately four finger widths from her wrist. She holds her fingers there for a moment then moves them below to Lawren's clavicle, off center from her sternum. After holding this position for a while Emelie reaches down and puts pressure on the inner area below her ankle. Lawren lifts her head. "I feel better now." She proceeds to stand up. Emelie fills a paper cup, made out of recycled paper, with water and hands it to Lawren to drink. "Keep hydrated." Lawren's color has returned to her face.

I ask Emelie. "Where did you learn those techniques?" Emelie replies, "It is part of your fourth-degree teachings." "There are sections of the fourth-degree teachings?", I ask, "What are the other sections of teaching?" Emelie makes direct eye contact. "Of course, you must know how to render first aid, especially after learning Defensive and Offensive tactics. You must be able to give medical attention to those you have injured by these tactics." She laughs, "Offensive Tactics are only used as a last resort. We don't believe in lethal force, unless all else fails AND you are in grave danger. You will learn other important information about being a whitch. Your powers will become stronger as you study and practice. The teachings will help you manage your personal powers and the natural energy of the universe."

We make our way back out to the patio. The animals are still there. Edward is sitting with them and feeding grubs to the mole. "Holy Moley says that the Darksiders partied a little too much last night. They used some hard drugs and Odious did not fare well. Moley tells me he was acting agitated, talking in a very low, deep voice and not making a whole lot of sense. In the past, when we didn't know much about psychiatric disorders, we used to believe people with these types of symptoms were actually possessed by the devil." Lexa pipes in "That's my vote." Edward continues, "Now we know that these are symptoms of a psychiatric disorder rather than possession. These symptoms disappear when the supposed possessed person is given psychiatric medications. It's only been recently that we discovered illicit drug use damages the brain. It's really sad that our nephew is showing these signs."

Lexa asks, "Is there a treatment program for addicted dark witches?" I was waiting for Edward to identify some rare herbs he uses to treat mental health and drug issues. He replies "Yes, it is called sobriety. However, the Darksider's culture encourages drug use and once they get entrenched in the culture and addicted to these drugs, it is very hard to intervene." Luciana speaks up, "When someone takes drugs, their brain actually changes and they lose their natural ability to produce their own chemicals their brain needs to function properly. I could get all technical and talk about neurotransmitters, receptors and metabolic pathways but I won't. I'll just say, Say No to Drugs but we know it's not that simple." Edward sighs, "It's just better not to use drugs in the first place, but, yes, it is just not that simple." Harley coughs nervously and pops a breath mint into her mouth. She fidgets then lights a cigarette but promptly puts it out in her effort to "just say no" to her addictions.

I return to my dorm. I open the door to dorm #9 and turn on the light. The dorm seems empty except for my suitcase on wheels sitting next to the door. I walk over, unplug the small refrigerator, and then turn down the heat. The mattress lays bare except for a bundle of dirty linens at the foot of the bed. I flash back to my senior year after graduating from Safehaven. I felt the same way that day when I cleaned my dorm for the last time. I was sad to leave this dorm room, even though I was looking forward to my new life as a graduate. I was leaving the dorm as a different person than when I arrived. I had so many new experiences during my years at the university. These were the most profound years of my life. I feel this way again. Over the last several days I have learned and changed. I'm not the same person I was last Friday. So much has happened. I have learned about myself, my family and my potential. A new door has opened and the metaphorical room has been totally remodeled. I'm not in the same house I was before. I can't say I'm used to the layout but am pleasantly surprised by the retrofit. Who knew?

I look back at the small dorm room as I turn off the lights and slowly close the door behind me. I feel sad as if I am leaving something dear behind. I feel pain in my heart. This still feels like my home and it hurts to leave. I miss the old Safehaven and the new Safehaven that includes my new-found family and powers. I roll my luggage with difficulty down the dirt path that leads to the Safehaven College parking lot. The wheels freeze up and make indentations in the dirt as I pull it. The others are waiting for me. They are sitting

in the back of Edward's 1941 red Chevy pickup. I feel Sam kneading inside my shirt. She doesn't seem sad to leave.

Edward looks back to make sure we are all settled in the bed of the truck before he puts on the gas. Emelie's head falls backward due to the force of gravity. The others cheer. I don't respond due to my state of grief. Tears well up as we head toward the parking lot at the other end of the campus. My eyes focus on the long, wood sign at the edge of the parking lot that says "Safehaven College." The same sign where I took my graduation pictures, thirty years ago. At that time, my dad and sisters were with me, celebrating my accomplishment. I long for simpler times when things felt secure.

I look across the bed to see Harley smiling at me. I see Lexa, laughing and making jokes. Juni's hair is moving in the breeze. Lauren's green eyes are focused upward in appreciation of the blue sky. Luciana is talking about her research project. I look toward the cab. Edward and Emelie are quietly talking to each other. I realize that this is not a sad moment but another one of life's perfect moments. A moment I will always remember because I am with the most important people in my life and we are all happy and healthy. There will be other perfect moments but for now this is one of the most perfect moments. I know I'm in good company and I'm with family.

We reach the edge of campus. The red Chevy slows then comes to a complete stop. Lexa jumps out first then lowers the tailgate. She lifts Susy out of the bed. Lexa grunts with effort as she does this. Susy oinks and tosses her head back in a playful manner. Lexa unlocks her car and Susy jumps in and sits down in the front passenger seat. She snorts and looks out the window. Lexa pushes a button and the window on the passenger's side slowly rolls down. Susy sticks her snout out the window, breathing deeply, enjoying the smells in the air. Her eyes narrow with pleasure.

Harley is holding her hummingbird's nest in one hand and pulling her luggage with the other as she walks to her car. She gets into her little white hybrid sedan. She ties the nest to her rear-view mirror. She pushes the ignition button. Her car is so quiet, you can't tell it's running, except by the stereo powering up. The broadcaster announces, "This is NPR, your National Public Radio. Next is Health Focus and we will be discussing alternative healthcare. Today we are comparing Holistic healthcare to Allopathic healthcare to see which approach gives the most care for the cost." Harley turns down the radio. She smiles in our direction and puts on some round framed sunglasses. She lights up a cone of incense and puts it in her ash tray. The smell of Patchouli wafts our way. I breathe deeply, taking in the aroma.

Luciana jumps down from the bed of the truck and holds her hand out to help Lawren down. Lawren grips her hand and gently lowers herself to the ground. Luciana runs to the passenger side of her red, concept car that was engineered at the Vehicle Research Department at Tucker College on campus. She lifts the passenger side door upward. This design is reminiscent of the Delorean car from the early 1980's. She holds onto Lawren as Lawren kneels down to get into the low bucket seat. Luciana hands her a bottle of water with electrolytes. She unscrews the top and encourages Lawren to drink. Lawren obeys and toasts all of us to say good-bye one more time. Luciana throws Lawren's luggage behind the seat, as the car does not have a trunk.

Juni points and presses a button on her key fob. Her red coupe rental car automatically starts and the parking lights turn on. She takes off her nicely ironed white shirt and hangs it over the back of the driver's seat. Her windows come down allowing the pent-up hot air inside her car to escape. She yells out the window, "I will miss convoying with you, Big Buddy." She frowns then smiles. She looks over to the wooded area behind the parking lot and scans the area but appears disappointed. She shrugs her shoulders in resignation.

I'm standing beside the Chevy with one arm around Emelie and the other around Edward as we watch the others get into their cars. I realize it is my turn to depart. I feel so comfortable between Edward and Emelie that I don't want to leave. My head tells me it's time to leave but my heart ignores the commands. I realize everyone is waiting for me, so I slowly withdraw my arms from behind their shoulders. Hesitantly I walk toward my SUV. As I approach the back bumper, I read my bumper sticker. It says, "My other broom is a scooter." I laugh at how accurate this bumper sticker has become. I throw my luggage in the back then walk around to the passenger's seat. I put a blanket down on the seat then I carefully take out Sam from inside my shirt and place her on the thick, fluffy blanket. She looks up at me, meows, kneads the blanket a couple of times then lowers herself onto her stomach with her legs tucked beside her. I'm proud that she wants to be my cat. Every time I look at her long black hair and big yellow eyes I melt. I pat her on the head.

Lexa puts her all-wheel drive sedan into drive and slowly heads out of the parking lot. Harley, Juni, Luciana and Lawren, then I follow her. We wave as we pass by Emelie and Edward. One by one music is turned up in each car. All different stations. I turn up my radio. The song Tapestry by Carole King is playing. "My life has been a tapestry of rich and royal hues, An everlasting vision of the ever-changing view. A wondrous woven magic in bits of blue and gold. A tapestry to feel and see, impossible to hold." I think about my life's ever-changing view and the richness of my experience over this weekend. "...Once he reached for something golden, hanging from a tree." I think about burying the ashes of my grandmother under the pear tree, The Tree of Life. "And I wept to see him suffer, though I didn't know him well." I think about Sid and how he is trapped in his anger and suffering. "In times of deepest darkness, I've seen him dressed in black. Now my tapestry's unraveling; he's come to take me back. He's come to take me back." I shudder as I think about the danger over the last several days and the Darksider's jockeying for power. I wonder when there will be retaliation.

The caravan heads out of the Safehaven District and down Mystics Drive. Juni heads the other way toward Interstate 5. We pick up speed and the wind blows through my car. Sam seems undisturbed by the wind or the speed. She happily purrs and kneads the blanket she is lying on. I look down on the floor where my mother's study materials are sitting. I notice the book on top has opened to page 34. I shut the book so the pages don't get torn in the wind. Shortly thereafter, another breeze flows through the car. I look down and notice the book has again opened to page 34. There is a poem on this page. I lean down and close the book. I accelerate and turn up the volume of my stereo. When I look down for the third time, the book is open to the very same page. A chill goes down my spine. I pick up the book and put it under my leg, placing pressure on it as I drive. This will keep the book from opening in the wind.

I look ahead to see brake lights as each car brakes in the caravan. I'm slow to respond due to my distraction with the book. Further up, Lexa appears to have slowed to reminisce as we pass the nudist beach. I look to my right and my mouth drops by what I see. Near the water is Sid sitting naked on a rock with Odious and Nefara standing naked nearby. Lexa honks loudly several times, mocking them. I sink down in my car seat as I go by, hoping they don't recognize me. Harley sticks her hand out of her hybrid and flips them off. Odious turns around when he hears the honking. He looks up toward the highway but has a blank expression on his face. I accelerate and speed by.

I look at the vast bay, the blue sparkles caused by the wind and sun on the water. I smell the fresh air that has been ionized by the turning of the waves and the salt water. There is a sweetness in the air from the evergreens. A warmth radiates outward from the sand and rock on either side of the highway. There is a streak of motion overhead. I follow it as it passes me and continues in a straight line in front of me. It slows down several cars ahead and hovers above Harley's car then appears to drop down in a controlled movement. Suddenly I realize it flew at the speed of a hummingbird. The bird must have found its nest that was hanging from Harley's rear-view mirror.

I think of all the fond memories I have of Mystics Drive, Safehaven District and Baypoint and how Safehaven College changed my life. There has been so much opportunity and rich experiences since college. I feel fortunate to be able to relive my college years every June at Wasgard University.

I glance in my review mirror. A 1960's style bus has come up behind me. I expect to see Shirley Partridge in the driver's seat. It looks like the same bus I saw on campus this weekend. It stays back, keeping its distance but continues to follow us Southbound down Mystics Drive.

My cell phone beeps indicating reception. Although I hate to leave Baypoint, it will be nice to be back in Cedar Crest. I'm excited to see my children, my sister, my cats and our new family dog. I follow the caravan as it speeds down the narrow, winding highway. I look forward to my four-degrees of teachings through the coven. It's only three months until the Fall equinox.

The End

And a start of a new beginning

5% or more of the profits go to Fairhaven College to help support its unique style of learning.

www.ingramcontent.com/pod-product-compliance
Lightning Source LLC
Chambersburg PA
CBHW070322120726

47909CB00008B/2554